LOVE BY THE RIVER

It started as a gentle kiss. There was no passion in it at first, almost only a rite of recognition of their mutual feeling for the history of this place, and of each other, but it was a long kiss. Slowly it changed, until his mouth on hers and his hands on her back pressing her closer to him blotted out the night, the river, and the buildings behind them. Cassie let herself forget them, thinking only of the ever-deepening pressure of his mouth against hers. She wasn't sure which of them ended the kiss. She knew that neither of them wanted to end it.

San Antonio
Seduction

Louise Colln

PREMIUM PRESS AMERICA
NASHVILLE, TENNESSEE

San Antonio Seduction by Louise Colln

© 2006 Louise Colln
Published by Premium Press America

For information on Premium Press America books,
call 615/256-8484.

ISBN 1-933725-47-8

Design by Armour&Armour
armour-armour.com

First Edition 2006
1 2 3 4 5 6 7 8 9 10

For
Lindsey, Colln, and Marshall

1

"HERE I AM. I did it. I'm here. San Antonio, you belong to me. River Walk, you're mine."

Cassie Rogers ignored the fact that actually she owned only a little space on the River Walk and actually she didn't own that space, but only leased it, and actually she was in an unbelievable amount of debt in order to be in it. Today she was sole owner of her world, and she knew that every single person who strolled the gorgeous River Walk would visit Teddy Bear's Christmas Shop as soon as she opened her door for the first time right now. She let her thoughts tumble happily through her mind in a magnificent unruly heap.

She twirled in a celebration dance, feeling her short dark hair lift as she spun, and being careful to not knock an ornament off one of the Christmas trees that took the place of the shelves that had never arrived. She almost wished she were wearing a swishy skirt to twirl instead of the white button shirt and black pants she had chosen to be her sales uniform. But it didn't matter. She was here. She was opening her Christmas Shop right on the River Walk.

Since childhood visits from Dallas, Cassie had carried a wild love for the River Walk in San Antonio, especially at Christmas time. She loved the mélange of scents and sights, the lights twinkling from buildings and tall trees along the tiny San Antonio River, music sounding from bands or lone musicians scattered along the Walk, the odors of food cooking in riverside restaurants and being served at outdoor tables, enticing strollers. Most enjoyed specialty menus at the tables, but Cassie's best memories were of finding take out to carry to the tops of bridges, of watching boats full of tourists float under her, of listening to a minute or so of the boatman's spiel of historical facts, interspersed with corny jokes. Occasionally a boat filled with a local choir would drift by, offering up good, or not so good, but always enthusiastic, caroling. At other times, she would talk her parents into sitting for a while on wide concrete steps or on iron-framed benches with ice cream cones. Always, a feeling of joy seemed to rise from the friendly water to be reflected back from the tourists crowding the sidewalks.

Cassie pulled herself from her memories of the past and her exuberance of the present to the down-to-earth, frightening fact that when she opened that door her career in the business world was on the line. The door was more than symbolically open to success or failure, depending on who chose to come in.

She took a minute to look out her oblong front window, to make sure that the tall man who had twice knocked on her door wasn't there, thank goodness. She didn't allow herself to think of anything attractive about his strong-featured face and powerfully built body, or the fact that his knocking didn't cause her to feel any alarm. Though she had remarked to herself that she suspected he had a WILL WORK FOR FOOD sign behind his back, she had felt an odd sense of comfort in his presence. But no one, absolutely no one would she allow into her shop until opening day. Today. Right now.

As she turned back to look over her well-lighted stock of big, fluffily dressed dolls, teddy bears, and Christmas ornaments of all sizes, Cassie could feel the smile on her face and knew there was a glint of determination in her blue eyes. She took in a deep breath. She would succeed. She was here. In San Antonio. On the River Walk. She couldn't repeat that enough.

At least she was barely here. The shop had been stripped by the former tenant, and the shelves and display stands that Cassie ordered put up were still somewhere in some warehouse. The man who kept promising to install them seemed to dissolve into the mist even while talking to her. And she was ignoring that rather large drip from the cold faucet of the basin in her minuscule workroom till she brought in money to pay the unbelievably high cost of a plumber. The new amber-colored rug that was required to replace the stained poison green one left by the previous tenant had cut into her available funds more than she had planned, and left her with little money. She didn't dare even consider that the shop might be anything but a success.

Determined to not let anything slow her down, she had scratched her hands putting together artificial Christmas trees, hung her decorations and figurines on them, and placed the trees about the shop with walking space between them. She'd sprayed them lightly with pine scent so everyone, especially every woman, who came in would stop and breathe the air with a look of surprised joy and remembrance on her face. She kept one tree behind the others, close to her register counter, empty. She would cover it with miniature, stylishly dressed dolls as soon as the shipment arrived. Other dolls and bears too big to hang on trees, she placed in baskets or on whatever tables she had been able to find in the short time she had to ready the shop for customers.

Now she was ready. "San Antonio, come on in."

She danced to the door and opened it to let soft Christmas music float out toward possible customers, making a happy ritual of turning her make-believe wood sign to OPEN. She listened, enchanted, to the sound of a South American band somewhere down the river, and laughter from a couple holding hands as they walked by. She smiled greetings to a short, more-than-plump woman who came in carefully, turning sideways to walk between the trees, though even she had enough browsing space—and was that huge-gray-furry-thing some kind of Texas wildlife?

Paralyzed by surprise, she watched whatever it was saunter casually around the biggest tree that stood just in front of the Teddy Bear shelf near the door. She had bought that small shelf in a discount store, climbed a stepladder to install it, and placed a magnificent white teddy bear on it. Then she had painted a sign. "Teddy Bear's Christmas Shop," in squiggly letters for the door, and installed a smaller one just under the bear's shelf.

The monster was seriously contemplating the tree, as though deciding whether or not to try climbing it. Cassie left her customer wavering between a ceramic sugarplum and a tiny fruitcake and raced over, determined to stop whatever critter it might be.

Before she could reach it, the animal made a flying leap onto the tree. It seemed to stop for a minute, almost as if it suddenly realized that this wasn't a real tree. Then it crashed on up, using the branches like a ladder, and ignoring the shower of fragile ornaments hitting the floor from the shuddering tree.

Its head appeared near the top. With a final tree-shaking push, it leapt to the lap of the bear, turned around several times, and settled down. As the animal snuggled contentedly in the bear's lap, it folded itself into a neat oblong and looked down at her with the slightly tilted, very green eyes of a happy cat.

"Get! Shoo!" Cassie called, looking about for a broom or something else to prod it down. Then, realizing that if she did, it would probably come down by way of the tree, causing more damage, she stood in silent frustration, feeling her spirits filtering down like the falling ornaments. This was the absolute last straw. Why were these things happening to her wonderful new business?

And who was that very short person who had followed the cat in, who shouldn't be in here without a parent, who seemed to be caught up in something still hanging on the tree? A ceramic angel, if Cassie was reading the line of his gaze correctly.

The angel was one of only two that Cassie had been able to wangle from a nationally known artist. It was kneeling and looking slightly downward, the expression on its face a mixture of joy and tenderness. It was Cassie's most expensive and beautiful ornament, and she had admitted to herself, as she hung the two high above the reach of children, that she almost hoped no one would buy them so she could really own them herself.

"Doesn't anyone watch out for animals and children around here?" Cassie muttered, looking from the cat to the boy. Trying to decide whether first to go ahead and try to dislodge the cat or prevent the boy from crushing the ornaments that had fallen on the floor kept her paralyzed for a moment. The child hadn't looked toward his feet since he'd come in and seen the angel.

As she started to move toward the boy to firmly shoo him away, the huge cat suddenly stretched and turned in a full circle, letting his long fluffy tail swing down around a branch. The tree shivered several more ornaments off.

A look of pure surprise and joy lit up the boy's face as the ceramic angel fell in front of him. Without hesitating, he caught it up and ran out, cradling it gently in both hands. Cassie dashed out after him, taking time only to throw a baleful look at the cat, and moaning to herself about the customer who was watching with unabashed fascination.

The boy seemed to be heading for

the bookstore next door. A man stepped out of the store and caught him firmly within his arms to stop him outside the open door.

"Whoa, cowboy, what's the hurry?" he said, looking at Cassie over the child's head. Even in her annoyance Cassie was aware that the look was one of concentrated interest, and that he was the tall man who had attempted to make friends with her from outside her door. She came to an abrupt stop inches from the two.

"He's hurrying because he stole one of my best angels," she shouted, waving her arms with the intention of pouncing on somebody, anybody. The impression, as she skidded to a halt, that she had to turn her head at an acute angle to look into gray-green eyes slightly scrunched above fascinating lips that seemed to be trying not to stretch into a smile, made her angrier. "And an animal is in my store knocking things every which way and. . . ." Suddenly, she was trying to keep tears from her eyes.

"But I didn't steal it," the little boy insisted without moving his head from its place buried against the man's leg. "It just fell on the floor and I picked it up. It wants me to have it."

The man peeled him away from his leg and looked at him sternly. "If you took the angel without paying for it, Danny, you stole it. You know it's wrong to take something that belongs to someone else. Your mother has taught you better than that."

"But—"

"Danny, you have to give the angel back."

Danny, still cradling the angel in his hands, looked at Cassie. Now, Cassie could see that he was quite a handsome little boy, with neatly cropped hair and liquid eyes several shades of dark brown, framed by curled lashes that would have set any woman mad with envy. And his startlingly innocent gaze met hers squarely. She shut her mind resolutely from any attraction to him or the man, who must be his father.

The boy named Danny twisted so that his back was still firmly against the man's leg, and gave Cassie the full impact of his deeply serious eyes. "I'll trade you my skates for it," he said gravely. "They're good skates. Inline."

"Danny. You can't trade off your skates. Your mother worked a double shift to get them for your birthday," the man said. "By the way, I'm Mitch Williams. I own the bookstore. I tried to offer help earlier, but you were too busy to see me."

He reached past Danny to hold out his hand. Cassie started to ignore it, but then took it briefly, not acknowledging anything approaching friendliness. Something had to be done about the frustrated anger storming around in her head. Anger that almost shut out a discombobulating bunch of pleasant jolts swarming up her arm. She took in a deep breath.

"And do you know who that cat belongs to?" she asked, ignoring his expected response of her own name. "Someone has to make him come down."

He looked surprised. "Come down?"

"He's up on my Teddy Bear shelf." She didn't explain more. Never mind if he didn't know what she was talking about. She didn't want this man to know any more about her shop. The irrational expectation that he would somehow do something about the situation didn't bother her. Something underneath her anger accepted that this was a man who could manage a situation.

"Let's go back in your shop," he said. "A friend is watching mine. Come along, Danny."

Cassie found herself trailing them into her own shop. Inside, her customer had moved to another tree, from where she was silently watching the proceedings unfold. The cat was now sitting up, watching them with equal interest. Cassie had a weird feeling of being on stage in a very bad play written by a fourth grader.

"Now, Danny, we'll pick up the ornaments for Miss—"

She ignored his unfinished sentence and started hanging the ornaments back on the tree as they handed them to her. Danny worked diligently with one hand, still holding the angel in the other. Cassie noted with relief that only one ornament had actually broken against the carpet.

When they had all but the angel back on the tree, Cassie, annoyed that Mitch Williams hadn't taken the angel from the child, held out her hand for it.

"Let's go to the register," Mitch said, taking Danny's hand.

"Do you really think—?" Cassie stopped herself. It wasn't her place to tell this man not to reward his son for stealing, or, for that matter, how his wife would feel about that attitude of intense interest she was trying to ignore from him. She went behind her small register counter and pulled up the price of the angel.

The cat suddenly and gracefully leapt from the bear's lap to the floor and walked across to the legs grouped about the register.

Mitch Williams winced at the price but pulled out a checkbook. "And I make the check out to?"

"To Teddy Bear's Christmas Shop." She took perverse pleasure in keeping her name from him.

She watched the cat weaving happily from the small boy's legs to the long ones of the man.

"That's your cat, isn't it?"

He handed her his check. "Are you going out tonight?"

"Please, just take your cat and your son. You're giving me a headache."

"If you're not, come join our band. For the caroling. On the river. We rent one of the tour boats. Before Christmas.

December twenty-third, actually. He's not my son."

"Just—he's not?"

"Danny's mom sings with us. Little Bit's mine, though."

"Little Bit?"

"Him." He pointed to the cat, now slithering about the floor at his feet.

She stared at the cat in amazement. "That monster couldn't have been a candidate for that name the day he was born."

"Everybody is small once. You live over the shop?"

She nodded.

"We're double neighbors."

"Double neighbors?"

"Like when two brothers each marry two sisters and their children are double cousins. Well, anyway, I live over my shop, too, so we're neighbors upstairs and down."

She was silent.

"So, will you come to the band practice with me tonight?"

"Oh, no, I don't sing."

"You play a violin." He indicated her fiddle case, stashed behind her register table.

She shook her head, too surprised that he noticed the case to keep from answering him seriously. "I don't call myself a violinist. Just a fiddle player."

"We need a fiddle. We get together at Christmas time to play and sing on the river. We aren't anywhere near great musicians. It's just such a great experience to float down the river on one of the tour boats making joyful noise. You'll love it."

No way was she ever going to have any experience of any kind with this man, who was ruining her first day in business and forcing her gaze to keep returning to the My Book Shop logo stretched across the muscles of his chest.

She turned away. "I'm very busy. I do have another customer."

He turned a casually charming smile toward the customer, who responded with simpers. "Okay. I'm sorry about Little Bit. I won't let him come in again." He picked up the cat, draped him over his arm, took Danny's hand, and turned to go.

"Wait, I'll put the angel in a box."

Danny shook his head. "I don't need a box."

The infuriating man pulled Danny to a halt and looked back, grinning. "Tell me your name, neighbor. I want to be sure I'm speaking correctly when I call you Cassie."

Cassie heard a quickly suppressed snicker from her customer, who was following him out. To his store, Cassie surmised.

She decided to make a quick trip to the coffee bar on her other side for a takeout chocolate espresso, heavy on the chocolate

"Congratulations on your opening." Rosie Cline, the plump middle-aged owner of the coffee bar, expertly fitted a lid on a plastic cup of espresso and came out from behind her wide counter to bring it to Cassie, who stayed near her door. "Has it been good so far?"

Cassie caught a hesitation in her voice and wondered if she and how many others had heard her noisy race down the Walk.

"I—not really," she said, digging into her pocket for money, while watching the door of her own shop for anyone going in.

"I heard a little," Rosie admitted. "That man next door to you. Don't be surprised if he makes all kinds of trouble. I'm sure he's upset because you leased your space before he knew about it. He's looking to expand his store. I know it. His family's got stores in the East, and he's looking to open a branch here. You'll see. He wants my space, too." She gave Cassie a comradely wink before going back to take another customer's order.

Cassie took her drink back to her store, empty now of customers. She had learned enough of retailing in her mother's Christmas Shop in Dallas to be aware that opening a year-round Christmas Shop a few weeks before Christmas wasn't the best business decision in the world. But when she had learned through her mother's friend of an unadvertised space for lease, she knew that this was her time.

Now she had something else to contend with. Now she knew that Mitch Williams's pretended offer of friendship was only a cover for his real aims. Now she knew that visit from the cat wasn't accidental. But what about the boy? Had he been sent in there, too?

A wisp of memory of his serious brown eyes when he offered to trade his skates for the angel slipped through her mind. What a strange thing for a boy to want. In spite of herself, she was somehow touched by his passion, and intensely curious.

2

SHE WOKE BEFORE full daylight the next morning. After dressing while drinking a cup of black coffee she decided to open early. Some morning walker might stop in. Every purchase was desperately important to her. She poured herself another cup of coffee, and carried it down the narrow steps to her shop. Putting her coffee cup on the register table, she struggled for a minute with the quirky lock and pulled the front door open to customers.

An outsized envelope fell in on her foot. Intrigued, she bent to pick it up, at the same time feeling the river/sky colors pull at her gaze. Too enthralled to investigate the envelope, she walked to the sidewalk edge, looking up. A red rose sheen mounting upward on the sky seemed to cover the whole universe above her and reflect downward to the river until she had the feeling of being surrounded by the color of glory, watching the intercommunication between earth, sky, and river. Glass from surrounding buildings reflected glowing gold. The animated riverside restaurants were silent now, chairs and tables inside.

She stood holding the unopened envelope until the clouds faded to a soft violet, then a dull gray, as though such intensity had never occurred.

"Do you ever feel as if a new creation has happened just for you?"

Cassie jumped and frowned, not sure she wanted to let anyone, especially her troublesome neighbor, into the moment she had just experienced. "I didn't see you. How long have you been here?"

"A while. I was waiting for you to open but I moved away when I saw your expression. There are some moments we don't share with anyone."

She felt a flash of appreciation that he had brought her down to earth so gently, bemused that he could so exactly express her feelings, but not letting go of her memory of yesterday or of Rosie's warning. She held out the envelope, not allowing her expression to come anywhere near welcoming his intrusion into her time again.

"From you?"

"You could open it. There's an offer of a large prize inside."

She tore it open, expecting a large card from his shop, perhaps expressing apologies for the cat, but there was only a cheery Christmas paper napkin inside. She looked a question at him.

"You have to return it to claim your prize."

She held it out, curiosity keeping her from following her instinct to go back inside, letting him know she wasn't taken in by any hyped-up friendly action. He took the napkin and went into his shop, leaving her wondering what in the world he had in mind. Could he be playing a joke on the newest shop owner in the area? A mean type of joke with the end goal of making her not want to stay?

Without more thought she turned to go in. He would just have to learn that childish tricks like that, and like the cat yesterday, weren't going to defeat her. They would only remind her that his charm was totally faked.

Before she could carry out her determination, he returned with wings of the napkin peeping above an open box.

"The best coffee and muffins in the universe from the kitchen of Mitch Williams," he informed her. "See, if we sit here on this early morning empty bench we can tell if anyone goes into our shops while we eat and drink."

He seemed to be taking it for granted she would join him. What did she have to do to make him understand she wasn't interested in his phony friendship?

She didn't hold out her hand for the offered food, keeping her voice cold. "I need to be inside getting ready for the day. I can't afford to miss any sales."

She choked on the realization of her mistake. What she couldn't afford was to let him know how narrow a margin she was operating on.

He ignored her lack of response. "I want to make amends for the things that happened yesterday, and I can't think of a better way than to get you to sit down and really see the river," he said, carrying the box over and sitting down on the bench. He patted the bench beside him. "Actually, I lied. These really aren't the world's best muffins. They're frozen from the grocery. But the river is real. Even the color of the water looks better in early mornings."

Something held her, kept her from marching inside: the lingering serendipity of the sunrise and the river. How could she cut that short? Mornings like this were the reason she wanted to come to the River Walk. Was she going to allow this man to take them away from her? Besides, she wanted to dig beneath his façade.

She sat on the bench, well away from him. "How can I refuse such tremendous honesty?"

He totally missed the underlying cynicism. It was almost frustrating the way this man kept missing her jibes, and being—face it, Cassie—a person she'd like to know better, really better, if it weren't for Rosie and the cat. She almost choked on the idea that she was letting a cat help her decide how she felt about someone. Glancing over toward him, she just breathed a jagged sigh of relief that he had covered the store logo on his chest with a light jacket.

He gave her a napkin-wrapped muffin and coffee in a large white mug, and then let her eat in a surprisingly comfortable silence. When the muffins were gone and they sipped coffee, she let the silence and her train of thought push out a question about the odd behavior of the little boy who seemed so close to him.

"The little boy yesterday. Danny. Does he live nearby?"

He seemed to come out of a reverie of his own. "Do you know the history of the River Walk?"

She was silent for a surprised moment. He did have the most irritating habit of not answering questions, or of responding with a question of his own. "I only know that it's considered a treasure, and lots of people come to San Antonio just to experience it."

"And with good reason. But we have a group of women to thank for it. Back in the twenties, the city fathers wanted to cover part of the river and turn it into a sewer, but, thank goodness, some city mothers were wiser. Can you imagine this," he waved his arm in a generous sweep, "being a covered sewer?"

Cassie finished her coffee and set the cup back in the box. "Thank you for the food and drink. And the history lesson." She hoped he would hear her unspoken comment on his failure to give her the information she had actually asked for. "Now I'm going in to neaten up my shop."

Again she let the memory of yesterday speak for itself. But he only stood and took the debris from their breakfast to a nearby receptacle, then, with a cheery wave of his hand, went into his own shop.

Really, he could be most aggravating, she thought, even when he's being thoughtful, like letting her enjoy both the muffin and the silence of the River Walk before the daily throng hit it. Were Danny and his mother not to be talked about? She remembered that there was no mention of Danny's father yesterday.

Two women came into the shop, and she turned her mind to sales, letting only a brief blip of thought about Mitch Williams slip through her mind occasionally as she tended to a steady stream of lookers and buyers, grateful that this day was going much better than yesterday.

She half-expected Mitch to invite her to lunch with him, but she ate a sandwich alone in the dank room behind the shop, listening to the drumbeat drip of the cold-water faucet, and coming out twice to greet customers. Finally, she gave up and dumped the uneaten half of her sandwich, glad for the business.

She didn't see Mitch for the rest of the day, nor the cat, nor Danny. She tried to feel convinced that she was relieved, not lonely, as she shut up her shop and went upstairs to a frozen dinner, heated in her microwave.

The next few days he only waved to her once or twice from a distance. Was he giving her time to forget the bedlam of her first day in business? But Rosie in the coffee bar next door kept her fully aware of Mitch Williams's real ambitions.

"Believe me, he'll take over both our shops if we let him. Don't let that friendly down-home pose fool you. He's got folks in the East who can buy and sell half of the River Walk. Pretends to like spending time in that little bookstore so he can write some book he's working on. Likely story. Either he's been thrown out of that rich family up north or he's down here working for them." She didn't give Cassie a chance to talk before she added: "If you're wondering how I know about the family, my boyfriend's a private investigator. He did a little work for free. Or easy pay." She winked at Cassie, with a feisty glint in her eyes.

"I thought Mitch had been here for years. Actually, I thought he must have been born here. He seems to know San Antonio history, and"—she thought of Danny and that unknown mother—"he knows people. Like the band he asked me to join."

"Well, he was in the Air Force and spent some time at Randolph. And claims to have fallen in love with San Antonio. That book he claims to be writing is supposed to be on history and little stories about San Antonio. That band he's in gives him chances to meet people. And he's a people person. I'll give him that. Probably from being in the stores his daddy owns. Just don't fall for it, Cassie. You aren't going to be a part of that band, are you? He may find a place for you in it, just to wiggle his way into your thinking so you'll listen to him when he hones in on getting your space. Believe me, I'll live on my own bagels before I give him and his rich daddy a second word."

Cassie thought there was a question somewhere in the spate of words, but she left it there. Maybe she was learning something from Mitch.

Rosie hurried away to sell someone a

chocolate cookie, and Cassie slipped back into her shop, giving a suspicious look toward the logo outside Mitch Williams's store, not letting it remind her of anything about his body.

What was Mitch Williams after?

After closing her shop, Cassie went up to her apartment. She opened the refrigerator in the small living room/kitchen and found that, as usual, there was very little edible food in it. Somehow the shop left little time for grocery shopping. Moaning inwardly, she put together a sandwich and poured a glass of milk. Chewing the slightly dry cheese and bread, she opened her mail, finding a letter telling her that the shipment of miniature dolls she had ordered was delayed.

"As if I hadn't noticed that," she muttered, opening a recessed drawer in her little dining table and shoving the letter in with other mail that she could do nothing about.

She turned on the computer that took up half the space on the table she used more as a desk than a place to eat, intending to send off a brisk e-mail to the company that had finally noticed they hadn't shipped her dolls.

She checked her incoming mail first, thinking that perhaps something there might make her cheese sandwich rest more easily on her stomach. Seeing a message from her mom, she felt herself brightening up.

Cassie, Dear
I've already said I'm sorry we never got you that pony you wanted. And I yearly repent giving birth to you five days before Christmas. What possible other thing might keep you from communicating with your loving parent?

Mom

Laughing, Cassie put down the half-eaten sandwich and dialed the Dallas number she knew so well. She heard only two rings before her mother came on the line.

"This is your loving mother."

"Mom. How did you know it's me?" Cassie asked.

"Honey, I know just how to punch your guilt button, and I figured this is the time you'd be closing your new store and digging into your refrigerator for a cheese sandwich and milk. I was pretty sure I wouldn't have to go into the long pregnancy and painful birth routine."

Cassie laughed. "How do you know me so well?"

"Well I am your mother, and I did carry you all those months, you know. Also, I have caller ID now."

"You're going so modern."

She heard an exaggerated sigh. "Oh, how sharp as a dragon's tooth is a daughter who has her own business."

Cassie carried her phone over and settled comfortably on her couch, shoving a cushion into place. "I don't think that is exactly what Mr. Shakespeare said."

"Whatever. Is your silence by any happy chance because you've met Prince Charming or just that you're spending way too much time in your shop?"

Even the memory of opening day made Cassie have to stand up and pace the floor, moving through the narrow spaces between her furniture. "The first day I was ready to pack up and come home or hit somebody. That, I think. Hit somebody. There's this cat."

"Honey, a cat isn't going to turn into a prince."

"Well, this one wouldn't be a prince anyone could live with if he did. Remember those two angels that I was so lucky to get?"

"As I recall, you somehow managed to get them before I did."

"Hey, Mom, business is business. I learned at your knee."

Cassie smiled delightedly to hear her

mother's rich laughter. "So long as you learned fairness and honesty there, as I know you did. But there's more on the angel and the cat?"

"He climbed my Christmas tree." Cassie didn't explain the tree. She had already described her shelf woes and how she managed them. "This cat wandered in and climbed my Christmas tree and knocked one of the angels off and a little boy came in and stole it and when I chased him out a man, not his father, met us. . . ."

"Ah, now the man enters. Was he handsome?"

Cassie drifted back to the comfort of the couch. "Well, I guess he is handsome."

"A change of tenses. So he's still around."

"He owns the bookstore next door. But he brought the boy back in, and bought the angel, and I don't think he should, and the cat belongs to him."

Cassie hesitated, deciding not to go into the whole story. She didn't want her mother to suspect that her new shop might be in trouble already.

"Okay, you sold the angel. I agree that he shouldn't have rewarded the child for stealing the angel, but maybe he had a reason. You know what Pappy always said."

Cassie was happy to have the conversation skimming by her adventures in the shop. "No, Mom, which one of Dad's many sage sayings are you referring to?"

"Well, I think 'Just say nothing till you get all the facts' would fit nicely here."

Cassie had a moment of thankfulness that, though Julia Rogers sorely missed her husband, she didn't dwell on his death but enjoyed her memories.

Her mother brought her out of her thoughts. "Other than the cat and the angel, how is the shop going?"

"Pretty well, I think. Not nearly as

busy as yours in Dallas, but I'm trying to put all the tricks I learned from you into it."

"Good. Last question. Since you're canceling Thanksgiving this year. "

"Canceled due to lack of time. It's just another work day for Teddy Bear's Christmas Shop."

"So are you coming home for Christmas?"

Cassie sighed. "You know I want to spend Christmas with you, but I don't see how I can. I'll only close the shop on Christmas Day, and I can't afford to fly up. Up and back in one day in traffic would be murder."

"All right. This is just going too far. Missing Christmas with your old mother for the first time in your twenty-four years. There's only one thing to do. I will just have to drive down to San Antonio for a while."

"Oh, would you? I'd love that. I admit I've been a little sad about Christmas alone. I've been too busy getting the shop ready to go anywhere or meet anyone. Well, except for this band I'm thinking about joining."

Her mother groaned. "Not another man longing for Nashville. How do you do it, Cassie?"

Cassie laughed, and then became thoughtful. "Mom, you just have to understand that I'm over Ted in any sentimental way. I learned a few things. But it was a really good thing, because now I know that this is what I want. I appreciate that you made me practice my fiddle all through my almost-happy childhood, but it's just a fun thing. I don't want the music world. Just to make a success of this shop." She laughed. "That's a new thing, isn't it? It's usually the other way. The poor unhappy person longing to make music and forced to drudge in the business world. I'm totally happy in the business world, Mom. Didn't I really ever tell you that?"

There was a moment's silence on the other end of the line. "And are you going to join this band?"

"I haven't decided yet. I'm so busy with the shop. But getting out might be fun. And you know, I do enjoy playing that fiddle. It's the man next door. The cat man. But I don't think he's in it for more than fun, either. It's just a pick-up band he's invited me to play with. They're going to play on the river a few days before Christmas. A lot of groups do it here at Christmas time. Remember?"

Julia's voice showed that she had decided to let the question of the band go. "Well, you won't be alone at Christmas. In fact, I'll let Helen handle the shop here and I'll be there, oh, some-time before Christmas. I'll talk to Helen about it."

"Wonderful. I can't tell you how wonderful. I can use some of your smarts about this shop, but most of all I'll love to see you."

After she hung up, Cassie finished her sandwich, thinking how great it would be to have her mother visit. She knew her mother wouldn't interfere or comment on her decision to play her fiddle again if she chose to play with that band, or on the man next door. At least not openly.

On Sunday, Cassie didn't open until noon. She promised herself a morning to enjoy the River Walk like a tourist.

She made herself a cup of coffee and spread peanut butter on toast, and then she dressed in jeans and easy-fitting T-shirt and went out onto the River Walk.

She walked past the already busy restaurants, and those that wouldn't open till later. She stopped for a moment to listen to a not very good, but very enthusiastic, trio in church choir robes singing *Away in a Manger*, thinking that she hadn't heard the song since childhood.

After applauding politely, she walked up a flight of steps to the street, and crossed it to a bench in Alamo Park.

A South American calypso band was playing. She listened to it for a while, watching the old-fashioned carriages being pulled by horses clip-clopping down the street with happy couples or families inside. The horses seemed as comfortable ambling beside cars and trolleys as if they were alone on a country road.

Trying to put some energy into the day, she reminded herself that she still hadn't actually gone into the Alamo. She joined the people walking across to the building. The cobbled plaza and old stone chapel, all that was left of the original fort, brought a moment of nostalgia for the history and sacrifices of others, and then made her frown with the memory of Mitch's history lesson of a few days before. Was everything she did going to make her think of that man?

Inside the building, she tried to change back to the nostalgic feeling, but failed. A quick tour of the tributes and historical exhibits left her with an edge of guilt for not responding to it as the intense history that was there. Fathers and mothers trying to guide wiggling children into interest in the exhibits, answering questions, and talking in low intimate tones with each other made her more aware of being alone. She left, decided not to visit the gift shop, and walked a length of the River Walk for exercise, not meeting the gaze of other walkers as she usually would have.

Back in Alamo Park, the band had left, and she thought of her phone conversation with her mother. Ted Tenison had been a part of her life in Dallas for a couple of years. While working in her mother's Christmas Shop there, she had played her fiddle behind his singing in several clubs. But when he had announced his intention to take his guitar and head for Nashville, he didn't invite her to go along. Probably, he knew that she didn't have the fervent ambition for the music world that he did. To her, their gigs had just been fun. So when a friend of her mother's told them about the unadvertised space coming open on the River Walk, she jumped at the chance.

Now, sitting on the bench with tourists wandering around her, she put Ted away with only good wishes for his career in Nashville.

"This is what you really want, Cassie."

She was so intensely into her own thoughts that she was hardly aware of speaking aloud until a small girl walking by stopped.

"Are you a writer?" she asked, looking earnestly into Cassie's eyes.

Cassie smiled, shrugging away a feeling of embarrassment, and answering her as seriously as the child had asked the question. "No. I'm a business woman." She heard the happy pride in her own voice. "Why do you think I'm a writer?"

"My daddy is a writer, and he talks to himself sometimes."

The child went on to join her family. Cassie smiled at them as she saw the little girl explaining why she had stopped.

The fact that almost the first person she met in this creative part of San Antonio was interested in her fiddle was pure serendipity. She decided not to question her luck but accept his invitation to play with them, even if Rosie was right and he only wanted to get her space. She could take care of herself if that came to a fight.

Feeling sure of herself again, she went back to her apartment. An attempt to take a quick nap failed, and she happily went down to her shop. That was where she wanted to be.

Business was better than at any time since she opened. Tourists looking for unusual ornaments and door decorations kept her busy and the register buzzing. She was exhausted but elated when she put up the CLOSED sign, letting herself close early on Sunday. Unable then to stay in longer, she came out just in time to see the sunset scattered over the sky in rose-red bits and pieces, while directly above a partial moon floated beside a pin-point star.

She sat on the bench for a while, just to enjoy watching the cheerful families walking by. And the happy couples. She wasn't thinking any thoughts that Mitch might close shop and come out to watch the sunset and the people, even though company would have added to the enjoyment of the moment. But not his. She didn't care that he put up the CLOSED sign on his store and gave her a casual wave before striding off down the Walk.

Knowing the truth about him, or maybe the truth about him, the last thing she wanted was to have to act as if she thought his pretend friendship was real. Just because she was going to join his musical group didn't mean she was interested in him, only that she might enjoy keeping him hanging for a while about her decision to join. Let him ask her once or twice more.

She went up to her apartment. Wishing that she had thought to buy food while she was out earlier, she found a frozen diet dinner and microwaved it, remembering that she had forgotten to eat lunch.

3

"PLEASE FEEL FREE to browse. Let me know if I can help you." Cassie gave a young woman a Monday morning smile that, in spite of herself, felt forced. Monday had been her least favorite day since high school, and she could feel the Sunday euphoria rapidly leaking out of her mind.

She busied herself rearranging Santas on a food cart she'd found at a going-out-of-business sale. She'd turned it into a useful part of the shop by wrapping each shelf like a Christmas present. She had done the same with two old-fashioned wooden stepladders. The customer wandered around picking up items and putting them down or fingering decorations hanging on the trees. She stopped by the bare tree near the register counter, looking at it with a question in her face.

Cassie tried to give an upbeat answer to the unspoken question. "It's waiting for a shipment of beautiful little dolls to come in. I hope you'll come back to see them."

"If they ever get here," Cassie added to herself, as the woman gave her a vague smile and walked out.

Watching the first customer of the day walk out without buying anything, Cassie stiffened. Wasn't its being Monday bad enough? That monster called Little Bit was walking in the door, looking almost as if he was trying to sneak in while she watched the customer walk out. But his contemplative gaze at the redecorated tree beside the bear showed that if he thought of her at all, it was only as someone who placed interesting things in his ever-so-innocent path.

Cassie felt something screeching inside her. How could Mitch Williams let the monster come in here again after the mess he made of things before? Now she knew Rosie was absolutely right in her judgment of that man. He was obviously using the cat in his plot to drive her out of the space he wanted.

As the imp in cat's fur gathered his legs to leap, she dived forward and caught him in her arms, almost losing him as he wiggled his surprised fat body against her grip. She ignored the front claws raking across her shoulders and back, as he seemed to be trying to climb her like some version of the tree she was shielding from him. She encircled him even more tightly and managed to turn him around, to dislodge his claws from her neck, but determined not to turn loose of him until she had delivered him back to his owner, along with several pithy comments about where pets should be kept.

She wedged the cat's back legs as best

she could against her barely rounded stomach, pushing it out in the process so that she walked like a high school band member, marching a squirming bass drum across the football field at halftime.

They had barely reached the sidewalk when she caught a glimpse of a man in colorful kilts standing in front of a café a few doors down. The sudden screech of his bagpipes made both Cassie and Little Bit jump.

The cat splayed his legs and stuck his claws in her. The sudden pain playing like lightning over her arms and stomach made her jerk his upper body to arm's length. Giving himself a push off with his back claws against her stomach, he flew through the air toward the river like an improbable fur-bearing balloon. His splashdown into the river seemed to send waves that grew in Cassie's mind to a colossal size and sound.

Mitch came running out of his shop as the noise of the bagpipe stopped as suddenly as it had started. "Little Bit," he yelled. "What have you done?"

"He was . . . I was. . . ." Cassie declared, though she wasn't sure if the question had been directed to her or the cat. She stopped, as Mitch seemed not to be hearing her. He ran as close as he could get to the edge of the river, looking as though he might be trying to figure out some way he could jump past the shrubbery into the water to save the cat.

Cassie watched helplessly as Little Bit, who now showed them that he was capable of a low-grade style of swimming, struggled against the waves pushed up by a tourist-filled river tour boat.

The boat slowed. The boat driver stopped his historical narrative in mid-sentence. "I'll get him, Mitch," he called. He guided the boat over, expertly scooped Little Bit up in a long-handled net, and pulled him into the boat. The passengers on the boat laughed and waved cheerfully, in spite of the fact that the wretched cat was spreading water all over them. They broke out in applause as Mitch managed to get close enough to reach the net full of spitting cat, almost dropping him back in the water.

"I always keep the net close," the driver called in answer to Mitch's thanks. "People drop things out of the boat. Never caught a cat before, though. I'll pick up the net next trip." He waved cheerfully, his passengers now laughing and getting acquainted with each other as they discussed the miserable cat. Everyone was trying to outdo the others on why the cat was in the river, with laughter going in waves back and forth between them and the strollers who had gathered on the Walk.

Cassie, thinking that she owed him this much help, ran into her workroom and grabbed a big towel to take out to Mitch. Kneeling, he spread the towel over the net, which he now had on the ground, reached inside and pulled Little Bit out, bellowing and scratching.

"Can we go in your shop?" Mitch seemed to be taking it for granted that she was going to help him care for the cat, which was now making growling noises low in his throat, as Mitch folded him inside the towel. "My dad is watching mine."

A thought blipped through Cassie's mind that Rosie had said his father lived somewhere in the East. So that father was now visiting in San Antonio. To help Mitch obtain the space he wants. The plot is following Rosie's warning. She tucked the thought away until she could contemplate it later. At the moment, her stinging midriff wasn't leaving any free space in her brain.

The small crowd that had gathered began to drift away as Mitch carried Little Bit, totally wrapped into the towel so that he didn't drip, into Cassie's workroom. Only one woman wandered into the shop, and she called out that she would yell if she needed anything. Cassie left the curtain open so that she could see inside the shop. This was the kind of day that would encourage wandering customers to pick up small merchandise without paying.

She was desperately feeling the claw marks on her body now that the excitement was over. She stood watching Mitch's sympathetic care of the animal with a growing resentment.

"Why don't you keep him somewhere?" she asked.

"He stays in my store. He greets my customers. He never leaves the store."

She waved an arm. The pain that caused made her angrier. "Excuse me. He has left your store twice. To come into mine."

"I brought him down and left him at your door that day," Mitch said, not taking his gaze off the cat, which he was gently rubbing with the towel. "He's my dog."

"Hunh?" Could he be any more impossible than this?

"Some people use dogs to get someone's attention. You know, walk them on the beach or here on the River Walk. I used Little Bit since I kept failing to get your attention by knocking."

She rubbed the spot on her stomach that hurt the most, sorry now that she'd let him bring the cat in here. It was keeping her from inspecting her own scratches. And that cat's problems were more important to him than her injuries. Caused by that cat, she reminded herself.

"Well, you certainly did that."

He didn't look up from his gentle rubbing of the cat. "Did what?"

"Got my attention." She hoped he might notice that her tone wasn't friendly.

"I didn't mean to let him stay long. I was on my way to get him and be humbly apologetic so you'd notice what a nice man I am."

He looked up briefly with an appealing grin that Cassie suddenly realized she'd noticed every time she'd talked to him. "I thought it would give us something romantic to talk about while we sat in our rockers celebrating our seventy-fifth anniversary. How we met. I didn't guess what he'd do to your tree or that he'd fall in love with your bear, which I assume was why he slipped out again today and tried to go back to it."

Cassie choked on the massive whirl of sarcastic words fighting each other to be the first out of her throat. She gave up. The ridiculous statement about an anniversary didn't deserve a response. Besides, he was concentrating completely on the cat as though he wasn't aware of saying anything like what she thought she had heard.

Little Bit was now resting comfortably inside Mitch's arm, only his massive head sticking out from Cassie's towel, his eyes squinted into near-sleep.

Mitch's own eyes scrunched a bit. "But why were you were carrying him when he did that swan dive?"

"Can't you guess? I was bringing him back to you. Can't you lock him up or something?"

For the first time he really looked at her. "Cassie. There's blood on your blouse. Did he scratch you?"

"I think that if I took a drink of water, it would gush out of me like a cartoon." Cassie tried not to sound as if her middle was hurting as much as it was, hoping he would leave so she could look at the painful damage to her stomach.

He slapped himself on the arm. "What an idiot I've been. Little Bit is very important to me, but that's no excuse. I'll take you over to the hospital. Cat scratches can be dangerous. Let me see." He slipped his hand over her arm. "I'll pay for the emergency room if you need it."

She pushed the hand off abruptly. "Certainly not. I'm quite capable of deciding if I need medical attention and sending you the bill."

"Put a new blouse on it, too." That smile happened again, only this time it made her follow his gaze to the long tear in her blouse that extended to below the top of her pants. Followed, she realized now, the long burning raw throb that told her she planned to bend over and scream just as soon as he left.

He sobered, realizing that she was in pain. With another apology, he carried Little Bit out. Cassie heard his friendly remark to someone in the shop that she would be out soon. Pretending she couldn't feel pain, she pulled her blouse together, folded the bloody part under, and tucked it inside her pants. She went into the shop, where two very good sales helped her feel better about the pain but didn't reduce her anger with Mitch. The amused look her customers gave to her blouse told her that the excitement on the river had brought the ladies in.

So close to their leaving with their goodies that she suspected he was watching, Mitch came back in without Little Bit.

"Use this," he said, giving her a bottle of something and a handful of cotton balls. "It's antiseptic and soothing. I'll watch the shop while you go in and put it on. If the scratches are really deep you still need to get medical attention. Do you have a doctor?"

She answered with a glare. Now he was getting much too interested in her scratches, and the fact that she didn't have a doctor was none of his business.

Ignoring her less than friendly response, he propelled her with his hand on her back toward her workspace. She went in and pulled the curtain.

Inside, Cassie scrutinized her arms and stomach to find that none of the scratches was dangerously deep, though she knew that she would need to watch for any later infection. She daubed the solution on them and almost immediately felt a sting and then an easing of the discomfort. But she couldn't get to the scratches that Little Bit had left below her shoulders. She was trying to reach them by bending her arm behind her back when he called from somewhere near the closed curtain.

"I noticed that your blouse was torn in back, too. Just slip it off your shoulders, and I'll put the stuff on those scratches."

"No, thanks. I'll do it myself." Too late, she realized that her voice was telling him exactly of her straining contortions.

"Cassie, you'll be covered as much as most of the women on the River Walk. Well,"—he seemed to be considering his statement—"maybe not now but in summer. I've put the CLOSED sign up for a few minutes, and I'm coming in. Cat scratches can be dangerous."

She felt his hand moving her arm back to a more comfortable position, then sliding the blouse off her shoulders before he took the cotton ball and bottle of antiseptic out of her other hand.

"You know," he commented. "This whole operation would have been easier if you'd just removed the blouse before you started."

Cassie felt herself turning red with something between anger and embarrassment at his sensible comment. She wasn't anywhere near a prude and could feel perfectly comfortable in a bikini, but there was something about knowing that he was just outside that curtain that had made her keep the blouse on. She didn't want to consider why that should be, but she had an unhappy feeling that he knew exactly how and why she was having a delicate moment and was secretly laughing at her. She marked up another mental check against him.

She put such awkward thoughts out of her mind as the soothing feel of the soft cotton ball across her shoulders almost made her anger go away. Or be replaced by a response to his hands on her skin that seemed to be closer to a loving touch than a treatment, that made her think of how it would feel if there was no wall between their beds upstairs. If they were even closer than they were now. If. . . . She told her mind to shut up and jerked her head around ready to tell him to back off.

Her mouth streaked across his cheek. Instead of pulling back, there was an almost imperceptible feel of his mouth moving closer to hers. For a time that held them both captive, she looked into his eyes, fighting a need to feel his skin under her own hands. Then, sensing that his mouth was coming down on hers, she twisted her back to him and pulled the torn blouse up on her shoulders even though she could feel some scratches farther down that she hadn't allowed him to find. Perhaps she could manage to get to them later.

"Thanks for the stuff," she said, gathering up the cotton balls and holding them out to him. "Now I've got to get my shop open again. I don't want to lose any sales."

He waved away the cotton balls and handed her the bottle. "Keep it. You may need to use it again. You will tell me if you find a deep scratch. I'll foot the medical bill. It's the least I can do."

"No." She took long enough to finish her statement to be sure he took it in. "The least you can do is keep your cat away from my bear and everything else in my shop."

"Right. I'll tell him." He sounded as easy as if she had just invited Little Bit in any time he felt the urge to visit her bear. On the way out, he flicked the sign to OPEN.

She felt annoyance rip through her mind again that this man wouldn't respond in kind to her remarks or answer her questions. How could she have been so unlucky as to get him next door to her shop?

The memory of that near kiss, and the knowledge that she had felt the urge to get closer as much as he did, made her even angrier. She forced herself to remember that, all the while he was forcing his hands on her (well, honestly that wasn't quite true) that her shop was closed and his was open. This man was doing exactly what Rosie had said he would do.

He had barely left when Rosie came in, so soon after he left that Cassie suspected that she was watching. Neighbors were certainly taking a great interest in her day.

"Cassie," Rosie called, "are you all right? I saw that monster jump in the river and hoped he'd drown, just to get even with that man for the nasty things he's doing. I'm just waiting for something to happen in my business. Monkeys to come in and eat my bagels or something.

Can I do anything to help? Jim's taking care of my customers. That's my boyfriend. He helps me when he's not doing anything in his detective business. He makes a coffee drink that doesn't have a name yet, but people come back for it. Well, actually, he calls it a purple pineapple puddle even if there's no pineapple in it."

Rosie was sliding her bulk between the trees as she made her way back to the workroom, talking all the way. Cassie honed in on her offer to help. If she could get that low scratch taken care of, she could make it through the rest of the day. The one too low down to allow Mitch to treat it.

"Just that one down here," she said as Rosie's body filled the doorway, already clucking at the sight of Cassie's shoulders.

"It's not as bad as it looks," Cassie said, moving to make room for Rosie in the tiny workroom and feeling jammed between the work table and the wash basin and the boxes of replacement merchandise lining the walls. Rosie seemed not to notice as she lifted Cassie's blouse and took cotton balls and lotion from the table.

Rosie's gentle massage of the lotion into the scratch was soothing, or perhaps it was that the last of the scratches was medicated. Or the constant run of Rosie's fuming words about the maneuvers of the Williams clan may have given Cassie more mettle to take on the fight.

"Now I'll just watch things while you go up and get another blouse on. No way you can meet customers in that." Rosie flipped her hand at the blouse.

"You're right." Cassie looked at the torn blouse, feeling her anger at Mitch feeding on the thought of the need for a replacement. Who had time to go shopping, to say nothing of the cost? She recognized that she was becoming illogical, since Mitch had offered to pay for a new blouse. She didn't voice her thoughts to Rosie, who seemed to be waiting for bits of rancor to feed on.

Cassie grabbed up the container of cotton balls and the lotion and put them behind the register, thinking she would discreetly apply the stuff to a couple of scratches on her arm for the rest of the day. With a quick word of thanks to Rosie, she ran up to her apartment to change her blouse. She was ready to open to the world when she came back down.

She followed Rosie to the door and double-checked the sign to be sure Mitch had actually left it at OPEN. Seeing several women coming in a group, she hurried to pull the curtain to the workroom, promising herself to clean it up later.

APPLYING THE SOOTHING liquid to her scratches that evening, she mused that they were feeling better and her sales had been the highest yet. She chose not to think that they might have happened because of the cat incident. But she took pleasure in thinking that she was way past failing in her first few days.

She woke once in the night to apply lotion to her scratches, wishing curses on man and cat probably sleeping soundly on the other side of that wall. But most of the pain had subsided when she woke. The scratches seemed to be drying up. She dressed in her usual pants and blouse, considering whether to send Mitch Williams a bill for the ruined one then deciding she didn't want to think about it.

She took the stairs down to the shop two at a time. This was a brand-new day. No way could it be as bad as yesterday. She opened the door at the foot of the stairs with a confident smile on her face.

The rug squished around her foot as she stepped into the shop. It felt like stepping into a big wet sponge.

She stood with one foot on the rug

and one on the stairs, looking down at an elongating soggy stain that was seeping under the workroom curtain and running over toward the empty tree.

She pulled her foot back up to the step and simply stared at the mess for a moment. Then she found a spot to walk on and pulled the curtain back, feeling the wet hem clutching against the floor. She wasn't sure if that pressure in her chest was from holding her breath or tears she was too distraught to cry.

The old fashioned handbasin had a groove on each side where the water was dripping out. At least it hadn't got to the point of gushing over the sides. The grooves had sent it in two narrow streams under the door and into two of the boxes against the wall. Thankful that she kept several towels in the workroom, Cassie grabbed a couple and flung them on the plastic-covered floor, one stopping the water from the door to the shop and one against the boxes.

Ignoring the slick floor, she plunged her hand into the basin, wincing as she pushed out a minor wave of water. She jerked her hand out at the clammy feel of something spongy clinging to her fingers, then frowned, looking through the water at the heap of cotton balls jammed against the bottom of the basin. Overnight they had clogged the drain enough to over-flow the tiny basin. Cassie pulled the cotton out, almost getting some enjoy-ment from watching the water gurgle down the drain. At least they hadn't got so far into the drain she'd have to call a plumber to get them out. She squeezed them in one hand and dropped them into a trash basket, while grabbing yet another towel with the other.

The towel soaked up most of the water in her rug as she stood on it, applying pressure with first one foot and the other. The second towel left only a damp stain. Thank goodness the cus-tomers wouldn't be coming back here to the empty tree. Perhaps it was just as well that the undelivered dolls weren't hanging there. She checked the wet boxes, unpacking undamaged ceramic candlesticks in one. The second one was worse, with several candles coming loose from wet plastic wrappings.

She left the merchandise crowding the table and turned the boxes upside down to dry, rather than take time to carry them to a trash bin. It was way past opening time and the CLOSED sign was still hanging on her door. So much for this being a new day.

But that wasn't the big question. The cotton balls in the basin were the big question. Leaving the workroom untidy was a big no-no, but she had been in too much discomfort at the end of the day to do more than race up the stairs as soon as the last customer went out, undress, and apply the lotion.

But how did the cotton balls get into the basin? By the hand of that person next door? The table in the minuscule workroom was close enough to the basin that the used cotton balls could have been pushed there in a single sweep of someone's hand. Accidentally or on purpose?

She decided to think about it later. Even if Mitch hadn't done it on purpose, the fault had to be laid at his door. At his ownership of that animal.

But it wasn't possible to accuse someone of doing such a tawdry thing without sounding paranoid. If he was going to use his father's money to scare her out, surely he could think of bigger things than cotton balls in a basin. When he came over later to ask how her scratches were, she answered him coolly, and let it go at that.

"It's high noon in Texas and you should eat."

Cassie looked first at Mitch's feet as he walked over to her perch behind her register to be sure the cat was nowhere near, then let her gaze wander past the well-fitting chinos and open-collared shirt to that mouth, which kept forming itself into a smile that probably made some women want to touch his lips with their own. She jerked herself back from wherever her thoughts had taken her to realize that he was talking as well as smiling.

"I've learned to adopt an old Southern custom of closing at noon. Though I don't actually take a siesta. One must keep the rent paid."

He's kidding, she thought. *He's forgotten that he said his father is here and can watch his store. Rosie, you're right. He's using silly little tricks to make me lose sales.*

"And I want to make up for Little Bit's bad behavior," he added.

She decided to go along with him. Her scratches had healed over the past couple of days with no infection, and she was ready to play his game and win. "If I asked how Little Bit survived his adventure would you actually answer?"

"Of course. Why would you suspect

that I wouldn't answer? There's this little outdoor restaurant down the way. Want to try some German food?"

"German? In San Antonio?"

"Actually, many of the people who settled San Antonio were German. German settlers came over in the mid-nineteenth century. They were the dominant people then."

Cassie was surprised into a semi-friendly question. "Do you teach history?"

He shook his head. "Just a buff. Researching for some writing I'm doing."

Cassie, thinking that he had almost given her an answer to a question, didn't respond to the writing remark, remembering what Rosie had said. A lot of people liked to play like writers.

She mentally congratulated herself on her newly acquired ability to put a certain level of coolness in her voice. "Interesting, but I still don't want to close." No point in telling him again how little loss of trade it would take to make Teddy Bear's Christmas Shop fail.

"Then I'll go down and get take out Mexican. I'll help you watch for customers while we eat. I promise not to drop any sauce on the floor. And I'll make it all disappear if a customer comes in."

Obviously he wasn't stupid. That irritating failure to hear the coolness was as infuriating as his earlier failure to hear the angry heat in her words. It had to be purposeful. Maybe he liked to see the red that had flushed her cheeks since childhood at any high level of emotion. The knowledge that the red was there frustrated her more.

But she was hungry, and it was true that the scent of hot food from the riverside restaurants had been teasing her for an hour, keeping her from her uninteresting sandwich back in the workroom. Why not let him ply her with food?

When he came back, she pulled back the curtain to her work area and watched him set the food out on the skinny work-table. She watched his eyes carefully to see if by any guilty chance he let his gaze slide to the basin, but he didn't. Cool character or innocent person? She had no answer.

"We can sit on these. They're empty." She pointed out two wooden boxes, and he pulled them up to the table. She took a mischievous pleasure in knowing before they were seated that the boxes, which were right for her, were ridiculously low for his long legs. He managed to sit on his box by pushing back from the table as far as possible against the cardboard boxes set against the wall and resting his elbows on his bent knees. Being careful, she noticed, not to push against the boxes hard enough to break any fragile orna-ments inside.

"Have you thought about our band?" He handed her a taco and offered sauce. When she shook her head he poured it liberally on his.

"I haven't had time to think about anything but getting this shop up." She might as well annoy him a bit by appearing chilly about joining the band, even though she knew she was going to join. He seemed eager to get her only for her fiddle, she reminded herself, grinning inwardly at being able to frustrate him. He was so good at frustrating her. Besides, the more time she spent with him, the more chance to find out what he might be planning for her and for her shop.

They didn't talk for a few minutes, both busy trying to eat tacos that were breaking up in their hands with some kind of grace. He was bending forward, holding his taco between his knees with a napkin under it to catch the dripping sauce. He met her gaze, and they began to laugh. Suddenly Cassie felt almost comfortable and able to enjoy the delicious meat stuffing in her taco.

He finished his taco. "Think about

it. It's a pick-up band, but we enjoy ourselves. We've got guitars, horns, and whatever else someone can play. They don't even have to be good. Just enthusiastic. Do you play your violin often? I haven't heard you."

"Fiddle," she reminded him.

Those gray-green eyes glowed softly as he grinned. "Exactly what we don't have. Exactly what we need. Please come."

She balled up her napkin and stood up. It felt good for once to look down on him. "Thanks. Maybe sometime."

He stood immediately, his face pleasantly solemn, as though he wasn't aware of any upmanship. The fact that she wasn't sure if he only stood as some kind of gentlemanly action or to never let her have the symbolic upper hand irritated her more.

"Tonight? Tonight is sometime. You can practice with us."

"Tonight?"

The temptation was playing against her desire to turn him down. She had missed the music, the camaraderie of other amateur musicians. Perhaps she had played coy long enough. She might be frustrating herself for the pleasure of making him beg. Besides, the more time she spent in his company, the more she could judge his motives.

"All right." Then, before he could answer, she turned away. "Oh, someone's coming in. Stay and finish the rest of the food if you want."

Mitch left soon after, giving her a wave of the hand that didn't carry the debris of their lunch. Cassie was thankful for the excuse to leave him and concentrate on the woman who was seriously contemplating a gracefully wide-coated Santa, a big one.

She would go with him tonight for the pleasure of the music, but she wasn't ready to spend more time with him than necessary to find out what was really on his mind. Not while the accusations of the woman in the coffee bar were on her mind. She was going to analyze every friendly overture he made.

4

"I'LL COME BY for you when we close our shops." Mitch stopped just inside the door of Teddy Bear's Christmas Shop. "I'll meet you outside your apartment. I'll give you exactly fifteen minutes to change from your working clothes. We meet in a garage."

"Oh. I'll feel at home. We . . . I practiced in . . . a friend's garage in Dallas."

If he noticed her hesitation in talking about her earlier musical experience or anyone attached to it, he didn't mention it. She thought she heard an irritating under-his-breath chuckle, but he only added, "This garage is special. It's close enough to walk if the weather's nice. Oh, wear old jeans."

She hesitated, almost tempted to change her mind about going anywhere with him. Didn't he know she'd pick up that nasty snigger at whatever he thought he'd heard in her comment? Now he was trying to dictate what she should wear. Then she decided that she wasn't going to let him deprive her of a chance to play her fiddle again.

She simply ended the conversation with a question, beginning to enjoy a mind game, counting how long it would take her to get one answer from him. "Oh, and how did Little Bit survive his experience?"

"Little Bit sits on my counter."

Well, she supposed, changing her frown for a smile at an incoming couple, in a way he had almost answered a question, but she couldn't count it as a score on her side of the game.

After she closed and ran up to her apartment, she took five of her fifteen minutes debating whether to let him tell her what to wear. Then, deciding he probably was only making sure she would fit in clotheswise with the rest of the musicians, she went with his suggestion and slipped into jeans and a rose-colored pullover sweater. She changed the loafers she had worn all day to lace-up walking shoes and ran down to the shop to pick up the fiddle she hadn't remembered to bring up earlier. She was just in time to meet him on the street outside her apartment.

The weather was lovely. It was just cool enough for a sweater as they walked under the streetlights through the still busy streets. Mitch waved frequently to a cop on a bike or a driver of one of the old-fashioned carriages, pulled by patient horses that plodded happily along the streets. Once they stopped while he fed a chunk of apple from his pocket to a gentle spotted horse that was standing at curbside, waiting for passengers. Cassie thought the horse seemed to know him, as it responded to his pat on the shoulder by searching his hand with its mouth. The driver stood by, grinning.

"Do you want to feed Anabel?"

At Cassie's nod, he brought out another apple slice wrapped in a half-sheet of writing paper and handed it to her.

"Do you have anything else in your pocket?" she asked in amusement.

"Anabel's waiting for her apple. Just hold it out in the palm of your hand."

Cassie unwrapped the apple and held it out, enjoying the feel of the horse's soft lips snuffling the apple from her hand. After the horse had taken the apple, Cassie began to smooth out the paper, aware that there was something written on it. Mitch took it from her hand and carried it, wadding it up as he went, to a nearby trashcan.

"It's just scribbling," he said when he came back. "Just an idea I had."

"For your book? Are you writing a

book?" she asked, remembering Rosie's comment.

"Sometimes people bring me stories. About San Antonio. We need to move on. We'll be late."

He turned several corners, and Cassie was somewhat disoriented before he stopped in a commercial neighborhood. Where, she wondered, was the garage they were to meet the others in?

"Here." It was almost as if he answered her thoughts as he led the way to the open door of a commercial garage. "It's this garage. Benny Karcher plays sax. He owns the garage. Be careful walking through. The floor gets a little greasy."

"It's this garage? With oil and grease and broken cars?" She was watching her feet, glad she wore heavy treaded shoes that wouldn't slip easily.

"Why did you think I suggested old jeans? We'll come in the waiting room door next time. But I want you to meet someone. Benny." He spoke to a small man with disorderly hair who was grinning at them from the yawning front of a battered-looking car. "I've brought you a gift. This is Cassie Rogers, fiddle player. Cassie, Benny Karcher."

The little man slammed down the hood of the car and came toward her, with a wide grin that no one could have resisted. Cassie didn't even try. She liked him already.

"Welcome, Cassie. You'll like me better if I don't shake hands. I've been working late. The owner of that car wants miracles and wants them yesterday." He held both his grimy hands wide, and they all laughed. "Mitch, just go in the waiting room and get drinks and stuff out of the machine. Or there's coffee, but I made it this morning. I'll be right in after I wash up." He punched a button, and the wide door behind them slid down.

Inside the waiting room, Cassie accepted a soft drink but refused the peanuts Mitch got from the machine after digging through all his pockets for change. There were the usual plastic chairs set haphazardly about the square room with torn-apart pieces of the day's newspaper scattered about. Seeing that Mitch was placing the chairs in positions for the practice, she helped him set them into a casual circle, without asking if he wanted her help.

They had just finished when three others, two men and a woman, came in. The men were dressed alike in jeans and T-shirts, but the woman showed off her stunning legs in minuscule shorts. It was only after noticing her unbelievably long legs that Cassie registered the rest of her body, wrapped in a top as tight and abbreviated as the shorts. Just for a minute, Cassie wondered what the woman would wear if it should get chillier.

Cassie sat down abruptly, almost wanting to hide her own appearance. Had Mitch told her to wear the old jeans she was now feeling frumpy in just to let this woman dominate the men, or was he really concerned about getting oil on her clothes? She frowned at him, but he was too busy being entwined by the siren—who certainly wasn't concerned with any smudges on the small bits of fabric she wore, or on all the skin that seemed to stretch out in all directions—to notice. Cassie had an unwelcome blip of memory of the feel of Mitch's hands on her own skin. She shoved it firmly back into delete, where it was going to stay.

The taller of the two men busied himself getting out his guitar, seeming to be trying not to notice the woman's embrace of Mitch. The other one watched with his head half-turned away, an unreadable expression on his face.

"Mitch, why haven't you called me?" the woman asked, looking as if she was trying to get closer though, in Cassie's opinion, it wasn't possible.

Pulling slightly back from the woman's

tightly pressed body, Mitch nodded to Cassie.

"Nerina." He partially unwound her. "This is Cassie Rogers. Cassie, Nerina Smith."

Cassie hoped she managed not to let her thoughts show in her expression, as she acknowledged the introduction while trying not to look too closely at the two of them. Then she realized that Nerina (that name certainly didn't go with the pedantic Smith, and few parents would put a name like Nerina on an innocent baby) had already turned back to Mitch.

"She isn't the reason you've neglected me, is she?"

For once Cassie appreciated Mitch's habit of not answering questions.

He managed to finish unwinding himself from the limber Nerina, leaving her standing in a pout, and cuffed the shoulders of the two men as he introduced them. "Keith Thomas plays guitar when he isn't fixing cars for Danny, and

Ian Weaver plays a bunch of instruments, but mostly plays guitar for us."

Each of the two men held her hand a bit longer than necessary. It was almost as if they, each in his own way, made a special effort to bring her ego up a notch. Keith, leaning from his way-over-six-feet height, gave her a shy smile reflected deep into his eyes, while the shorter Ian came across immediately as a people person, with a welcoming remark and a grin that gave the impression of extending clear up to his cropped reddish hair.

Cassie responded to each of them while noting silently that all their effort would still have left her ego beneath the car out in the work area, with the long-limbed Nerina in the room. Then she rebelled at her own thoughts. There was never a day, even in her teens, in which she would want to imitate this woman, who must think that getting a man's attention was the most important thing in life, and that it could only be done with sexy clothing. Didn't she know that women had their own lives now? Nerina Smith must be living back in the days when women only sat on rocks in the sea and tempted men like Ulysses. What kind of ego problem was she hiding, this Siren From the Sea?

Cassie backed out of those thoughts. Nerina Smith's role wasn't her problem, nor was the woman's obvious goal to devour Mitch.

She was surprised when Danny came in with a woman who looked old enough to be his mother. And who, in a much simpler way, was as beautiful as Nerina, though almost the exact opposite. She was dressed in classic pants and tucked-in shirt that made Cassie suspect she hadn't had time to change after picking up Danny directly from whatever work she did. The clothes fit her well, neither hiding nor highlighting the somewhat-beyond-slim curves of her body. The elegant bun she had fashioned her dark hair into added to the impression of just-off-work. Cassie let herself play a guessing game that work wasn't in an office; she wasn't sure why. She didn't get any further than that before the scene in front of her interrupted her.

Mitch deftly eluded Nerina's arms and immediately went into those of Danny's mother. Why, Cassie wondered, did he choose to bring another woman into the mix? Was he looking for a harem? Well, it would be a long day off, like never, before she wound any arms around him.

He kept his arm around Danny's mother and brought her over, introducing her as Sarah Marchiano. Danny gave her a self-conscious grin but said nothing before sitting down with a book. Sarah's response was as warm as Nerina's was chilly. Her friendly handshake made Cassie feel enthusiastically welcomed.

Benny Karcher came in, and they quickly settled into what was obviously a well-known routine. The men invited

Cassie into their tuning huddle, and she felt an immediate bond into that special intimacy of musicians everywhere.

It soon became apparent that Mitch and Sarah would do the vocals. They moved to a corner of the room to go over the carols they chose to sing, and Nerina stood beside Mitch paying no attention to anything. She didn't act as if she was going to sing with them.

"We'll do our version of *Joy to the World*," Sarah said as they joined the others and chose chairs. "Cassie, just come in when you see where you fit."

Cassie just listened the first time they went through the song, laughing softly to realize that it was the song that had a bullfrog named Jeremiah, and then she asked them to do it again. This time she put her bow to the fiddle, but kept her sound soft, underlining the voices. Their expressions told her they approved.

They went through several songs, both traditional and new, doing the classic *Joy to the World* after a bit. The men invited Cassie to join them in some instrumentals. Finally, they played old Texas cowboy songs. Nerina got up and danced, not well but seductively.

"We now need to induct Cassie into the Hardgravel Group," Ian said as they were putting their instruments away after agreeing to meet again in a few days, "and that requires a visit to the neighborhood square dance place. Who's in?"

"Come on, Mitch." Nerina wound herself around Mitch like a poison ivy vine. "We'll find a corner while they do that dancing thing they do to induct her."

Cassie put her fiddle in its case. "Thanks. I'm pleased to be brought in so quickly, but let me take a rain check on the square dancing. It's getting awfully late now, and I open early. But," she added, "I do mean I want to go later. I love square dancing."

"Me too," Mitch said. "I'm glad to know that you do, Cassie. This is a family place they're going to visit. Like in England or Ireland. Families come together, kids and all. Everybody who's learned to walk dances." Mitch unwound Nerina so easily that Cassie thought he must have had a lot of experience doing that. "And I walked over with Cassie, so I'll go with her," he added to the others. "We'll induct her later."

"Mitch, I remember the way home," Cassie said, being careful to put a note of irritability in her voice. She wasn't sure she really could get home from there alone, but she could always hail a cab if she got lost. She certainly wasn't going to keep Mitch away from his Siren Who Should Be Sitting on a Rock in the Middle of the Sea. "I'll be fine if you want to go with them," she added, careful not to mention Nerina's name.

"Hey, I'll take Cassie home." Ian sounded eager, turning his face-lighting smile on her.

Mitch took a slow inventory of Ian.

"Ian, Cassie is new in town. She's not ready for your Texas Two Step. I'll take her."

Cassie thought they were having a friendly bashing, but she wasn't sure if it was something else. She couldn't tell for sure. But Ian winked at her.

"I'm really the best of Texas and totally dependable. But I'll let you get to know me gradually." He turned to Nerina, while that unreadable expression that Cassie had noticed before slid across his face. "Nerina, you'll just have to make a toast with us. Come along."

Nerina's lower lip looked about two years old, but she walked out in her high heels in front of the two men. Cassie tried to promise herself not to ask any questions about her, but she knew she would. Eventually. But not of Mitch.

"Mitch, just shut the door when you leave," Benny called, following the others out. "It's on automatic lock."

In a moment Cassie, wondering why

they weren't leaving for home when the others went out, heard motors starting. One had the roar of a motorcycle.

"Benny," Mitch said, looking at her expression. "He calls that cycle his baby."

Cassie wondered briefly if she might get more answers from Mitch by letting him read her mind. Then she answered herself. No way was she going to let this man into her thoughts.

In a moment, she understood why they had stayed behind when Sarah brought Danny over to her. She pressed Cassie's hand warmly. "Danny has been waiting to say something to you."

She motioned for Danny to stand and held him in a one-armed hug while he apologized for taking the angel. "And I know that it really was stealing, and I have to keep the cards neat for a month in Mitch's shop and wash dishes for Mom all year to pay for it."

He looked proud and pleased rather than unhappy, and Cassie wondered again why he wanted the angel so much. It didn't seem the sort of thing that a seven-year-old boy would want. She remembered his bewildering offer to trade his skates for it. Perhaps he wanted it for a present for his mother, but obviously not a Christmas present, for it was no secret. Still, she felt that she shouldn't ask, and no one offered any more information as they waited for her response.

She hesitated for a moment, while thoughts raced through her mind of her own desire to keep the lovely angels for herself, and that it was only her need to recoup the cost of them that forced her to place them on the tree in the first place. She didn't understand why a boy of Danny's age would have such a strong need for the angel, but she understood the emotional response the angel created. There was just something spiritual about that angel, and the companion one that she still had.

She ignored the slim hope that Danny

was going to return the angel and gave him the smile she felt he had earned. After all, she had been paid fairly.

She wasn't sure what to say but finally came up with, "I understand, Danny," thinking all the time that she had just been telling herself she didn't understand. But she did recognize the strong response the angel invoked, whatever he planned to do with it, so she felt that she was being essentially honest with him.

Danny's grin widened and became the rogue happiness of a little boy as he relaxed visibly against his mother.

"Thank you," Sarah said, squeezing Cassie's hand once more. "I'm glad you're going to join us in our band. Your fiddle is going to make all the difference in the world."

Mitch reached out to hug Sarah easily, including Danny in the embrace. "Good singing tonight, Sarah. We'll wow 'em on the River."

Watching them, it was easy to see

that, no matter what Mitch's relationship with Nerina might be, he and Sarah had only a deep friendship.

Sarah laughed. "You know the tourists just applaud us because they feel sorry for us. We're so few."

"Not when you sing, Sarah," Cassie said. "I got goose bumps when you sang *O, Holy Night*."

"You should hear her when she gets all the emotion of the night on the boat," Mitch said, smiling down at her.

"I do get a little over-emotional." Sarah chuckled. "I always cry after we finish," she added.

After offering to drive them home, and being turned down by Mitch without his giving Cassie a chance to decide, Sarah and Danny got into an elderly sedan and waved as they drove off.

Cassie waited while Mitch tested the lock on the waiting room door. The door to the service area was already closed. They walked back through the now-quiet streets.

"I like Sarah," she said, and then wondered if she sounded as if she were asking for information.

"I like her, too."

His openness reinforced her sureness that he was only expressing friendliness. She decided not to comment on her impression of Nerina. The title Siren From the Sea ran through her mind again. Then she realized that he was adding a comment about Sarah.

"She's had some rough times." He didn't tell her any more, as if giving Sarah her privacy from someone who had just met her. He immediately changed the subject.

"I didn't take up her offer to drive us home because I love to walk in this part of San Antonio after the streets quiet down at night, and I wanted to share it with you."

Cassie's feelings from the music and friendliness of the evening, with the exception of Nerina Smith, kept her from the angry response she would ordinarily have to his making decisions for her.

He didn't seem perturbed by her failure to answer. "Will you come back to the band?"

Cassie was silent for half a block, and then agreed that she really wanted to play with them. His response told her that no matter what he wanted her to do in Teddy Bear's Christmas Shop, his pleasure for her part in the band was real.

He gave her a casual good night at her apartment door, but she saw from the corner of her eye that he waited until she unlocked her door and went in before going to his own.

"It's only because the music is pulling me," she told herself as she got ready for bed, later. "Just the music. Just the camaraderie of the group."

"Except for Nerina, The Siren From the Sea," she added just before falling asleep.

5

CASSIE HOPED THE tall man who appeared, smiling, in her shop almost as soon as she opened the door next morning would be a customer. The middle-aged man had a look of success and money as well as determination, and he might just buy half the store, she thought. Something familiar about his strong face niggled at her mind, though she couldn't quite place it. Torn between a judicious simulation of the recognition she felt she should have and an honest admission of puzzlement, she decided to settle for a simple "Good Morning."

Instead she heard herself yelling, "No. Not you again."

The man looked at her in a way that

definitely questioned her rationality. She didn't care. She wasn't going to allow that animal **in h**er store ever again.

Little Bit hunkered down in the doorway, hugging the floor beside the man's feet, perhaps as if thinking that he could make himself small enough not to be seen.

"Little Bit." She stopped for a moment, realizing that her voice had edged into the upper vibrations again. She raced toward the cat. "Even the ducking in the river didn't cure him."

Somehow that would have to explain the situation to whoever this man might be.

He turned to look at the cat. "He may have followed me," he said, calmly. "We're buddies."

Little Bit had stopped at the sound of their voices, still hugging the floor.

"No." Cassie forced her voice down several octaves, braking herself a scant foot from the two. "He's in love with my bear. He'll climb my tree and knock all the decorations off."

Then she absorbed what the man had said.

"You're buddies? With that cat?"

His smile got bigger as he nodded. The smile made her recognize why she had seen a familiarity in his looks even before he spoke. "And with his owner. I'm Owen Williams, Mitch's dad. I've been in San Antonio a few days."

Cassie nodded. "I know. You watched the shop while. . . ."

He smiled. "I heard that Little Bit went swimming. I apologize for not coming over to introduce myself sooner. I've been attending to some business."

Cassie didn't answer, wondering if his business was going to affect her own in a way she wouldn't like.

He looked at the bear sitting high up on its shelf. "I'll take the cat back to Mitch's shop. Then I have an idea. I'll be back."

He picked Little Bit up and went out, the cat hanging comfortably across his arm.

Cassie felt the need to lean against something. She went behind her register. Owen Williams didn't need to come back. Taking that cat home was all she wanted from either of those men next door.

But he was back in a very short time. He came to stand in front of the cash register, making Cassie feel as if she was barricading herself behind it. He might turn out to be as infuriating as his son, she thought.

"Here's what we need to do." He was covering the situation as seriously as if he were in a board meeting planning the next year for a big corporation. "It's obvious that Little Bit isn't going to give up his love for your bear, so. . . ."

"So he has to be penned up," Cassie finished, grimly. "Or perhaps sent somewhere else. Somewhere far away."

The man shook his head. "Mitch's

customers and friends expect Little Bit to be wandering freely in the store, and he's a very selfish, and very determined, cat. Penned up, he'd make such a noise no one would come near this part of the River Walk. So let's look at the other side of him."

"He has another side?"

He smiled. His mouth was shaped just like Mitch's, Cassie noticed. "Well, to be honest, maybe not. Change it to the other side of the question. Make a different way for him to get to the bear."

"I don't want him to get to the bear."

He gestured toward the bear looking down at them from his high shelf. "Think how your customers would react to seeing him sleeping in the bear's lap. Especially the kids. He might end up your best salesperson."

Following his gaze, Cassie reluctantly recognized the marketing concept and asked for his idea.

He moved his concentration to the

shop entrance. "First, we'll move that tree he used before over to the other side of the door. It's crowding the entrance a bit anyway."

Cassie nodded, admitting the fact.

"Then we set up two levels of flat space so that he can jump from one to the other."

Cassie grimaced. "My shelves still haven't been delivered. I've decided it's too late now to have them put up till after the Christmas trade anyway. Everything would have to be moved, and I can't afford to close for a day to get it done."

Again she wanted to bite her tongue, which seemed determined to let the Williams men be aware of how close to the edge she was operating. What a good signal that would be for them to move on her.

Owen Williams just nodded, seeming not to take notice of her admission, though she doubted that.

"Good thinking." He moved to the

area beneath the bear. "But we could get two shelves in here. Short ones. Lay them on a small metal frame, and fancy them up with figurines or such on the ends so he wouldn't knock them off and we'll be in business, so to speak. I'll find everything for you."

She waited a moment, digesting the wisdom of the innovative idea before finally admitting, "It would work, I think, but why?"

He winked at her. "It's the neighborly thing to do, to make up for all the alarm Little Bit has caused. And I like to make Little Bit, and my son, happy. Mitch and his sister are very important to me. His mother and I are divorced."

Cassie didn't mention that her mother was coming to visit. There was no reason to, she thought. They would probably never meet. Or if they did, Julia Rogers would be a great battle-scarred veteran of the retail wars to have on her side.

He left so engrossed in his ideas he

barely said good-bye. That afternoon two men came in and moved the tree without damaging a single decoration. They returned and set up the stepped shelves, adding several heavy ceramic sleeping kittens on the outside edges, and a discreet "Not For Sale" sign under the bear's shelf.

Cassie spent the rest of the day switching from suspicious questions about Owen Williams's real reasons for the plan to a business-level respect for his ability to carry it out so quickly. Once a niggling suspicion rose in her mind that the problems she had getting her shelves delivered might have their roots in the underhanded mind of the man next door. As well as the dolls that should be hanging on that bare tree in back, instead of somewhere in some warehouse, where the grim-faced Grinch refused to admit that they weren't going to be shipped before Christmas. Owen Williams's money certainly caused things to happen, and Mitch Williams would have access to that money.

Cassie couldn't keep from wondering why Rosie was so sure they were after her space. And why Owen Williams helped her own sales if he was after her shop. Didn't hard-boiled businessmen cut down on sales in any way they could when they were trying to force someone out? Wasn't that was the way they worked in the real world? But it was obvious that if Mitch wanted to expand, it would have to be in her direction. And Owen had said that his children were very important to him.

And why, if his father was so clearly moneyed and able to bring workers so quickly to her shop, was Mitch wasting his time in a tiny book and card shop? A first thought would be that he was rebelling against his family, but that was apparently not the case. So, was it true he was seriously working on writing a book? Or was he starting another dynasty in San Antonio, and did that dynasty want to demolish her small shop as quickly as his father had helped it? She realized that she had pursued the thought around a perfect circle. A circle that could easily wrap itself around Rosie's suspicions.

She went to bed that night, still wondering. Somehow in the night, though she couldn't remember any dreams when she woke, she seemed to have decided not to pursue those thoughts unless she received some kind of proof.

"But," she said aloud to impress it on her mind as she ate her toast. "I won't let myself be fooled. I'll watch. They won't slip anything past me."

Almost immediately after she opened the shop that morning, as though he considered the changes no more than his due, Little Bit showed up and jumped his way to the bear's lap. In the days to follow, business picked up as amused tourists told others and they came in to see the cat and the bear. Often she was asked if the sleeping cat was also a plush synthetic. In spite of the "Not For Sale" sign, she received many offers for either or both of them, which she refused with a smiling shake of her head as she rang up other sales on her register.

Rosie Cline wasn't impressed when she came over on Thanksgiving Day to see the display, holding a cup of something for Cassie. "On the house," she said. "It's my boyfriend's special purple pineapple passion. He's passing them out like candy this morning."

A thought flipped through Cassie's mind that the boyfriend never seemed to be needed in his office, wherever that might be.

Rosie set the cup on the top shelf of Little Bit's climb up to paradise and stepped back, close to an ornament-covered tree, to look at him. "Sure, the old man's helping you," she said. "And you've got feel good vibes about the business you're getting. So you'll be ripe for whatever offer he wants to make when he's still around after Christmas, taking care of getting whatever the crown prince wants. Well, let me tell you, I'll be reduced to living on my own coffee and bagels before I give him one good word."

She planted her hands on her hips. One elbow jiggled the tree hard, causing a couple of big metal horns to clash against each other. Little Bit woke at the sudden sound and came plunging down, almost missing the steps completely. Almost. Cassie made a wild dash to the cup sitting on his shelf, almost getting to it before Little Bit's back paw did. Almost. The cup took to the air in a graceful arc like a well-hit baseball and sagged against Cassie's feet as the top flew off and a horrible-purple-brown brew splashed across her feet, a goodly part of it hitting her pants, and dripping onto the carpet.

Rosie was there in a minute apologizing wildly. "Oh, Cassie, I'm so sorry. I shouldn't have set the cup there. I just wanted to see what the customers were so crazy about. I just meant to bring you something nice, and now look at what that cat did. Oh, look at your shoes and pants. He's a curse, that's what that cat is. A curse."

Cassie interrupted the splurge of words. "Just get a towel out of the workroom, Rosie. I'm afraid to move. I'll leave more marks on the carpet. The shoes aren't important."

She stood without moving while Rosie brought in a towel and put it on the carpet stain, stamping her foot on it over and over until most of the stain was gone. Enough, Cassie thought, that she could cover it with a figurine. Then she lifted each foot and let Rosie wipe her shoes. She slipped them off to be sure no more stains got on the carpet.

She gratefully accepted Rosie's offer to watch the shop while she went up to the apartment to change. After Rosie, still spouting apologies and comments about the cat, went back to her coffee bar, Cassie stood staring at what was left of the ugly purplish stain on the carpet, wishing there was some way she could move her business to a deserted jungle where the only neighbors she would have would be lions and snakes. People were so dangerous. Especially people who owned big, supposedly tame, wildly misnamed little house cats, and who, somehow, even when they weren't anywhere around, caused coffee to spill on her carpet because they wanted her to give up and move out of their way so they could. . . .

A man looking for a special ornament to make up to his family for being on a business trip came in, and Cassie stopped voicing mental suspicions to help him gather several. She was happily busy the rest of the day, without seeing either of her neighbors.

She declined Mitch's phoned offer to walk with her to the next music session at Benny Karcher's garage, without making any accusations about Little Bit that would have been laughed out of any court considering the way the accident happened, and certainly would have made him think she was being unreasonable.

She didn't want to talk to him about anything anyway, and conscious of his possible desire to end the evening with The Siren From the Sea, she drove her own little blue Bug to the garage.

Mitch was already there when she came in, and so were the other band members and The Siren. Dressed little differently from the earlier session. And managing to give an impression of being wrapped around Mitch, even when she actually wasn't. Determined not to look at them, Cassie chose a chair and concentrated intently on her fiddle.

"It won't help." An amiable voice spoke against her ear. She was pleasantly aware of a warm face close to hers, a body enjoyably in the personal space behind her, and a faint smell of some masculine shaving lotion. She turned quickly to find herself looking at the agreeable laugh crinkles around Ian Weaver's eyes.

"You really have to look at her," he added in a low tone. "She may not be tasteful, but she's there. She's definitively there." He seemed to take an overly long time looking at Nerina himself.

His pupils were slightly widened as he looked back at Cassie. She chose not to reckon with the question of which of two of them he was responding to, almost sure it was the long-legged Nerina. But responding, herself, to his friendly manner, she became brave enough to ask some of the questions squirming about in her brain. "I can see that she's there. But what, no, who is she?"

His grin disappeared as he became oddly serious. "A dancer, sometimes. You may have noticed that she isn't good. Someone who wants to be close to certain people." He nodded toward Mitch, who had casually returned Nerina's hugs then disengaged himself. Cassie suddenly suspected that Ian's earlier grin had been forced as he watched Nerina and Mitch. And there was that strange give-no-information mask that took over his face each time he looked at The Siren.

"But there's more." He nodded again, started to say something, and then seemed to change his mind. He didn't finish the story, if there was one to finish. With a final soft pressure on Cassie's shoulder, he found his seat and they all tuned up as Sarah came in, this time without Danny.

AT HOME AGAIN Cassie was aware of more questions than answers about everything that had happened since she arrived on the River Walk. And of thinking more of the Mitch and Siren questions than of the practice session, which had gone well. What did Ian Weaver mean by telling her that there was more, and then leaving it hanging? And did she care? She told herself that the answer was no, trying to drift off to sleep. Was it more that Mitch was starting another dynasty, as Rosie has said? Or that he was seriously interested in Nerina? And hadn't she already decided not to think about it anymore?

Eating cereal for a change the next morning, she suddenly remembered that she had dreamed about cats, lots of cats, sitting on huge rocks in the middle of the ocean. Each cat had its own rock to sit on. But where was she? She couldn't remember being a part of them on her own rock, but she was definitely there, perhaps hanging effortlessly above them. She considered the dream for a minute, and then decided it was silly. As long as the cats weren't wearing short skirts she didn't need to think about any possible meaning.

She had a happy number of customers after Little Bit made his daily appearance the next morning. She was concentrating so intently on her sales numbers that it took her a few seconds to recognize Ian Weaver when he appeared in her door. When she did she felt a surprising glow of pleasure as she returned his good-morning smile.

"I was just visiting Mitch for a few minutes, and I felt the need to start my day off with a glimpse of your face," he said, drifting easily into the shop and into a pleasant compliment.

Cassie looked at her watch. "Do you always start your day off this late?"

He answered casually, not showing any discomfort at a possible suggestion of questions of his lifestyle. "We were dancing too late last night, celebrating a new musical instrument in our little band and the new instrument player who keeps saying no to our invitations to go dancing with us. And we may have had a wee bit of drink."

Cassie squashed an urge to ask him how he made a living with such hours. It was pretty evident that the little bunch of amateurs she had seen wasn't going to do anything musically to bring home any cash. Unless they played on the street with a hat in front of them for tips. That was possible. Tourists, put into a romantic mood by the ambiance of the River Walk and the Alamo, weren't discriminating, and they had money in their pockets.

She waved her hand at the general area of the shop. "Some of us have to get up early. A middle-of-the-week night spent dancing might be fun but unaffordable just now."

He nodded. "So how about a middle-of-the-week dinner, ending early? Like this evening?"

Cassie shook her head. "I stay open until nine."

He grinned. "Okay. Nine it is. I'll pick you up here."

He was gone before she could explain that she didn't mean to give a time for dinner with him. But she turned back to arranging a new batch of tiny bears with an enjoyable feeling. Ian really was a nice man. She was glad to look forward to dinner with him.

True to his word, Ian appeared at her door just before she put up the CLOSED sign that evening, carrying a gift of one tiny orchid. Touched by the symbolic ambience of the flower, she pinned it on the shirt she wore as her everyday sales uniform along with easy fitting pants and low heels, thinking a bit wistfully of the fun of dressing for dinner.

"Looks perfect," he said. "But then almost anything would look perfect on you."

Cassie couldn't help laughing. "Even the outfits that The Siren From the Sea wears?"

"Nerina has her own way of defining herself. At least now. But why are you calling her The Siren From the Sea?" There was an intensity in the question that surprised her. As though he really cared why Nerina should be given that title.

He held the door for her then waited while she locked it. They stepped out onto the River Walk.

She stood still for a moment. "I sometimes come out here when I close the shop, just to feel free and look at the lights reflected in the river." Then she chose not to copy Mitch's fondness for ignoring questions. "I don't know why, for sure. Why I call her that. She just makes me think of The Sirens sitting on rocks tempting Ulysses and his men. A descendant, maybe." A snippet of remembrance of her dream slipped through her mind.

His smile was brief, and he didn't answer her. He waved casually at Mitch as they passed the still-open door of his shop. Mitch, who was behind his register, waved back, just as casually. Cassie was unpleasantly shaken by a blip of disappointment. It was totally apparent that neither Mitch nor Ian felt any discomfort at her dinner date with Ian. Had they made some kind of agreement that Ian would take her off his hands so that he could concentrate on Nerina? And why would she care if they had? Just in case, she determined to make it abundantly clear to Mitch that it wasn't necessary.

Nevertheless, she thoroughly enjoyed shrimp scampi in an outdoor café and found Ian's charisma not as superficial as she would have suspected, but an integral part of him. Her enjoyment lasted well through the meal and the slow walk up the steps to the street and to her apartment door, where he told her a modest good night with a quick kiss on her cheek.

"Was the food good enough to tempt you another night?" he asked.

"Very much so. And the company," she agreed as, with a quick squeeze of his hand, she slipped inside. She went to sleep relishing her memories of the evening and without thinking more than a couple of times of Mitch, sleeping on the other side of her wall.

6

MITCH APPEARED AT her door with a skim milk latte as soon as she flipped her sign to OPEN. Cassie took the cheering drink, wondering how Rosie responded to him when he went into her coffee shop to buy the latte. Did she let him know her suspicious feelings toward him or did she accept his custom graciously? And was he going to mention her dinner date with Ian last night?

He didn't. "I know we're pushing you, meeting so often for practice now. If you're too tired to walk to Benny's tomorrow night, I'll bring my car around."

She set the latte on her register counter and busied herself with a tray of small decorations that some child had examined too ferociously yesterday.

"It wasn't that I was tired the last time. I just didn't want to make you think you needed to come home when I did. So you'd be free to go dancing with the others." She kept her tone carefully innocent.

His face was just as expressionless as her tone. "Thanks," he said with no elaboration.

Cassie had the sensation of game playing. If he thought her remark was an opening for him to talk about that woman, that she cared anything about that woman or anything at all about his social life, he was wrong. Wrong. Dead wrong. She noodled her mind away from that subject.

"I'll see you later. Plan on riding with me tomorrow night. We appreciate having your fiddle in our little group. It adds exactly what we need, and you're good. You ever think of going pro?"

Cassie didn't answer. Maybe he would think she didn't hear him. Something in his expression told her he didn't think that but he was giving her the option of not answering. He changed the subject himself.

"You need to keep that tray of ornaments higher up."

With a friendly flip of his hand, he sauntered on over to his store, leaving her wishing she had cleared something up with him, but she wasn't sure what. For one thing, had she agreed that she wanted to ride with him? Did he know whether or not Ian Weaver had suggested taking her? Did he care if she would really prefer going in her own little Bug? Would she? Was she going to march over to tell him that she was capable of making her own transportation plans? On what shelf was she supposed to set that tray, since no shelves were delivered? Did he have anything to do with that non-delivery?

She turned to stare at the cup of latte

on her counter, as if it brought some kind of information from Rosie's bar, or could tell her if Rosie's accusations against the Williams men were true. She sometimes let those accusations get into her mind, especially when something went wrong in the shop, but she thought that she had been fair mostly, waiting for proof. She knew that if she ever should get proof that Mitch would do something so underhanded as to hold up her shelves, she couldn't even be as cautiously responsive as she was now. Not even for the camaraderie of the band and her pleasure in playing her fiddle. Or her decision to spend time with him in order to watch him and analyze his intentions toward her shop.

Her own sense of honesty wouldn't allow it.

Why not just get to work, and was that Little Bit freed from his nighttime incarceration and coming to visit his love?

It was, and he brought in a family with two children to watch him climb his personal mountain to his own paradise. The family, already having fun on their River Walk day, bought several decorations for their Christmas tree back in Missouri. Cassie wrapped them carefully in extra newsprint and watched as the mother deposited them in her practical outsized tote.

When they were gone, she walked over and stood below Little Bit. "Owen was right. You are a very selfish and determined cat, but I'm almost learning to like you for my bottom line's sake in spite of your disasters. Mr. Top Salesman. You've deserted Mitch for your own desires. Don't you feel any loyalty to him at all?"

Little Bit waved the end of his tail at her, turned to his side and went to sleep, his head hanging dangerously off the bear's lap. Cassie nodded. That position would please and entertain the customers and, while they were laughing, they would make the register ring.

Was Rosie just flat out wrong about Mitch's evil plans? When he was willing to share his cat with her? But Mitch wasn't actually sharing anything. Little Bit made his own choices.

And, she decided suddenly, so would she. She had been thinking that she might want to see what went on in that place the others went to after their practice. She would agree to ride with Mitch if he would agree to go to the square dance club with her afterward.

She wasn't surprised at how quickly he agreed. Or at how much she found herself looking forward to the evening, as she dressed in smooth-fitting pants with a belt and a tucked-in top embroidered with Texas bluebells. It was a shirt she had found back in Dallas, and one she had often worn to play with Ted's band. She always felt particularly pleased with herself when she wore it, and as she fastened her belt that pleasant feeling was with her again.

He knocked at her street door in jeans and open-throated shirt, and escorted her to a bright-red, two-seater sports car.

"The car?" she blurted out. "It's yours?"

"My only pet besides Little Bit," he answered, opening the passenger door with a grand gesture that told Cassie how much this one symbol of wealth meant to him. At least the only symbol she was aware of, not counting Rosie's allegations about his plan to get her space on the River Walk.

She hardly heard him add, "This one will do what I want it to do."

Her answering smile was a little belated, but he didn't seem to notice as he slid behind the wheel and guided the car into the street, making no attempt to show off its power for her.

Cassie decided not to tell him she had expected something like an old Chevy.

That might tell him that she had thought about him enough to analyze his probable tastes. She found the sling seat very comfortable and the short ride to a parking space in Benny's garage too quick to need any conversation.

Later, watching him over her fiddle as he sang with Sarah or leaned casually against a car that Benny had been working on, Cassie admitted that a woman like Nerina Smith would of course want to be close to him. Almost any woman would. Almost.

He made it plain that Cassie was riding with him to the dance, leaving Nerina to find a place with Ian and Keith Thomas and Sarah, who had ridden over with Ian. Nerina, it seemed, had walked from somewhere, Cassie decided, from the look of pure disappointment on her face now, with the idea of leaving with Mitch.

They took a while laughing and calling to each other as they fitted instruments and people in the two cars. Then Mitch led them several blocks to the dance. Benny waited to close up his garage before he followed them on his motorcycle.

"What's the name of this place?" Cassie asked, more to fill the car with some sound than for information.

"It's a family place. Help me look for a street sign. Never mind." He meshed gears smoothly. "We turn here."

It was barely more than a few minutes before he pulled into a large parking lot, about half filled with cars of all descriptions.

Cassie was pretty sure the building the dance was in had been built for something else—maybe a barn for the Texas cows and horses that galloped through all of the old Western movies. The round drink and snack bar just inside the door hardly seemed to take up enough of the space in there to be noticeable. Long tables spread out in the front and sides of the room left a wide space for dancing and, from somewhere in the dimness of the back, she could hear the crackling of a game on a TV. The bits she could hear of it sounded like a replay of some football game, though the cheerful arguments of the watchers were as excited as if they didn't already know the outcome.

The group headed for a table over at the side. They had barely gone through the friendly decisions as to who would sit where—and Nerina ended up beside Mitch—when a burly man appeared.

"Drinks on the house if you'll play a few. Summertime Band didn't show." He snorted. "Bunch of girls. They said they needed to sleep tonight so they could work—just because they've played the past five nights—well, how about it?"

For the first time Cassie noticed a small bandstand over by the door. Immediately afterward the men were standing and heading for the door.

"Is it a fire?" she asked Sarah. "Is there another door here?"

"No, and two in back," Sarah answered. "They're like a bunch of boys who're called off the bench at football." She laughed, indulgently. "They're going for their instruments. Yours must be in Mitch's car. He'll bring it in."

"Yeah, I had to come over with Keith." The sulking Sea Siren wasn't trying for friendliness.

Cassie became unhappily aware that the three women were alone at the table. She wouldn't have minded Sarah but just thinking of trying to keep any kind of conversation going with Nerina was causing something close to a headache.

They were all relieved when the men surged back in, motioning them over to the stage. Mitch handed her fiddle case to her and she busied herself preparing to play, and trying to not notice that Nerina came to the stage with them. To do what? Surely not to dance, and she had never shown any musical talent in the sessions she seemed to have attended only to be near Mitch. Cassie was pretty sure that Nerina's dances wouldn't go over well in this family place.

For the first two pieces Nerina stood off to the side of the band, only twitching her hips to the rhythm, while they played for a line dance. Men, women, and a few children came onto the dance floor with a two-tap step and lined up for a promenade. Cassie was surprised, even while enjoying the sight of the dancing families, that the children hadn't been taken home long ago on this school night. While playing the well-known tunes without having to concentrate on the music, she mused agreeably on memories of arguing with her parents at that age to let her stay just a little longer. They had insisted on taking her home early, even though they undoubtedly would have liked to stay for more sets of square dancing themselves. She was sure that there had been many more children here earlier in the evening.

Nerina stood quietly while Mitch and Sarah sang an old folk song, but a group of three men at a nearby table were already noticing her with obvious remarks among themselves.

Mitch and Sarah stepped back, and the instruments went into a down-home piece with a strong beat. Too late they realized it wasn't a good idea. Nerina moved to the front and started a body-flinging dance that brought the table full of men to their feet, yelling encouragement.

Perhaps Benny's idea of stopping the men by schlepping into *Danny Boy* wasn't good enough either. The men were coming up from the table, pushing their way through the dancing groups, before Mitch and Sarah could even start the lyrics. One man swung up to the bandstand and grabbed Nerina by the arm, attempting to swing her around in a semblance of a dance. The dance floor cleared, parents lifting their children up in their arms to carry them away from the coming brawl.

The music stopped as the men from the band dropped their instruments and surrounded Nerina and the stranger. They wrenched the belligerent man back to the floor and into the arms of the burly manager. More interested in protecting her fiddle than anything else, Cassie moved as far away as possible from the fight. She jumped at a touch on her arm, than nodded to Sarah. Together they slipped to the back of the stage.

In a few minutes, the raucous men were ejected from the building and a somewhat-nervous noise of talk and laughter came up again. Parents were gathering up their children and leaving, looking unhappy. Some said a few irate words to the manager as they went by.

He nodded and patted a shoulder here, an arm there, on his way to the bandstand. "Now play *Danny Boy*," he growled. "I was already thinking of sending those men home. They've never been in here before, and they don't belong in here. And if you ever let that woman dance again you're outta here for good."

Aware that their music was needed to bring back a calmer mood, they picked up their instruments. Benny chose a series of quiet tunes. Cassie surrounded Sarah's voice with low, sweet notes as she sang a few lyrics alone. Sometime during the fracas Mitch had taken Nerina back to their table and seemed to be shielding her from stares.

Seemed to be very protective, Cassie considered. Ian's words from the first night Cassie had joined the band ran through her mind. "There's more." She wondered again what he had meant. Chalk up another mystery about Mitch's intentions. Another reminder of the only uncertainty that made any difference to her—his intentions toward Teddy Bear's Christmas Shop.

The band played only a short while before going back to their table. Most of the people had already left. No one seemed to want to dance anymore.

Mitch leaned over Cassie's chair. "Do you mind if I take Nerina home? I know it's getting late." Though his words were apologetic, his voice wasn't.

"Oh, Mitch, I'm so sorry." She carefully poured honey into her voice, hoping a few bees clung to it, ready to sting. "I meant to tell you Ian is driving me home. That will free you for the Si— for Nerina." She ignored the fact that she would have to tell Ian that he was driving her home. She was sure he would agree that he had certainly meant to ask her.

Mitch's expression didn't change. "Then you'd better hurry." He gestured toward Ian, who was heading for the door, calling out a general "Good night."

"Oh, I'm going to meet him outside." If that smacked of a sort of secret rendezvous, so be it, and she certainly was going to meet him outside if she could get there before he left. But she was depressingly aware that Mitch wasn't buying it as she gathered up her instrument and raced out the door after Ian.

In the parking lot, Ian turned to her hail with a pleased expression that upped her ego a few degrees. But his lack of surprise that she wanted to ride with him, that he had actually been waiting for her, told her that Mitch had already made arrangements with him to take her home. Of course, she realized, Mitch wasn't a person who would just leave her to find her own way home while he delivered The Siren safely to her secret rock. But the fact that he let her do her— she now realized—silly little intimation of a secret rendezvous with Ian made her want to smack him.

When Ian ushered her into his faded Chevy, she understood even more Mitch's amused glint when she hinted at a rendezvous. Keith Thomas and Sarah were also piling into the car, saving a place for Cassie in the front seat. Benny Karcher waved a backward good-bye before he roared off on his cycle.

The conversation in the car was so self-consciously general it was painful, with awkward blips of silence before one of them came up with a subject away from the Sea Siren. Only Keith seemed not to be self-conscious about her. When he openly commented on her sleazy dance, no one answered, and he didn't pursue his thoughts.

Though she had somehow expected Ian to take the others home first, she was surprised when he drew up at her curb and simply waited in the car until she had unlocked her door and gone in.

Flicking the light to let them know she was safely off their hands, she undressed and prepared for bed in a quandary. Except for Keith, they had tried to sound as if the evening hadn't happened and Nerina Smith perhaps was a simple young woman instead of a Siren From the Sea. Cassie now saw her doing a less-than-elegant version of the hootchie cootchie on the rocks. No wonder Ulysses took so long getting home.

As she managed a fairly comfortable breathing space while covering her ears with a pillow that would keep any possible noise from next door away from her, she wondered if the others in the car started talking about what was on all their minds as soon as they drove away. Her last thought before sleep was that she was only half-accepted into the close group that met in Benny's Garage.

SHE HAD SEVERAL customers the next morning. Around noontime, resting on her stool behind the register counter during a lull, she felt a glow of pleasure when she realized that one of them was Ian Weaver. She didn't feel the need to stand, as she would have done with another customer. She simply felt a welcoming smile appear instinctively on her face as he leaned comfortably against her counter. He flipped a friendly wave to Little Bit, who had stood up and stretched at the sight of an old friend.

"I felt the need again to start my day off with a promised time with you," he said.

"Promised?" Cassie asked, knowing he must have visited next door before he came to her shop. "To whom?" She watched Little Bit settle back into his nap, perhaps feeling that he had done his duty by Ian.

"To me," Ian answered, with an easy grin.

Cassie decided to accept him at his word. She glanced at her watch without commenting on the time.

"And to explain to you that our little band doesn't usually have an evening like last night," he added.

She wasn't sure she wanted to talk about last evening's events. But he was here. What more was there to explain?

"Thanks for bringing me home," she said.

The friendliness in his eyes told her more than his words. "Anytime, Cassie. Anytime at all."

Maybe his eyes weren't telling her all that much. Was that twinkle really relief that she hadn't asked about Nerina's dancing? She remembered the stilted conversation in the car while they were bringing her home. She suspected that it became more personal after they left her, but maybe not. Ian could be keeping whatever feelings he had for the Nerina/Mitch thing even from the rest of the band.

Cassie wasn't sure that wasn't a swampy place to go. The group and their relationships was on the edge of bizarre. Except for Benny and Keith, they seemed to come out of nowhere on the nights they practiced. Sarah didn't give any reason for the times she rode to the garage with Ian or where Danny was while she was there. Cassie mentally agreed that she was under no obligation to do so, but she still wondered about the charming woman and her son.

The band members gave her a feeling of intimacy with each other but not yet with her, almost as if they were a family into which she was taken as a stranger who shouldn't be left alone for holiday dinners. And Sea Nymph Nerina seemed to be more of an intimate part of that family than Cassie herself showed signs of ever becoming. Because of Mitch?

Ian interrupted her thoughts with a smile that crinkled up his whole face, as he watched her intently. "You don't have to tell them if you don't want to. But I will give you a penny."

She had to smile back. "Does it require being with the group since birth to really be a part of it?" She felt herself blush. That wasn't at all something she had planned to blurt out.

He took a moment to consider it. Then she read the decision in his face to answer flippantly. "Or get to know one of us really well."

She decided to play along. "One of us?"

"Well, possibly me. In fact I come bearing gifts."

She looked intently at his empty hands, a mischievous grin playing about her mouth. She liked Ian.

He held his hands up, open. "Not physical gifts. Well, maybe I'm asking for gifts instead. Cassie, I'm officially offering you a chance to further your musical career. Will you go street playing with me tomorrow afternoon?"

She sobered. "Ian, you know I can't afford to close my shop in the afternoon." Then she grinned again. "Much as I've probably always dreamed of being a street performer."

"I picked tomorrow for a good reason. Sarah has tomorrow off, and she's always looking for a little extra money since her fool of a husband left her and Danny. She works in a dress shop, so she knows the ins and outs of taking money from customers, and she works for Mitch sometimes. She knows a lot of the people who come around. She can cover for you."

"Aren't you taking a lot for granted? Maybe she doesn't want to work on her day off."

A look of guilt crossed his face. "She asked me to sound you out about working here. And you do need someone to spell you occasionally."

"Why didn't she ask me?" This was another sign of an intimacy that she wasn't a part of.

"She's a little unsure about your feelings for Danny since he took the angel, and a little more unsure about your feelings for Mitch. Actually, I was supposed to feel out your response to the idea of having her come in sometimes so cleverly that you wouldn't realize I'm doing it. I failed on that, didn't I?"

"Miserably."

"Would you mind pretending that I didn't?"

There was no way she could not respond to his self-deprecating half grin. "If you'll answer something. Honestly. Are you really asking me to go street-walking with you—I mean—"

He hooted with laughter. "Guessing what the intended question is: I hope you will go playing music in the street with me. Will you?"

"Guitar and fiddle?"

"Right. I usually play the pipes when I play on the street, but this time it will be guitar."

She choked, and then giggled. "It was you, wasn't it? You scared Little Bit into the river."

He grinned. "It was me. I'm really sorry about the scratches. Playing the pipes takes a lot of concentration, and I wasn't aware that you were carrying him out till I saw him go in the river, then I waited to be sure he was rescued and decided to disappear for awhile."

"Does Mitch know?"

"Of course. He forgave me. Sort of."

She nodded, standing up for emphasis. "That does it. I'll be delighted to play music in the street with the man who dunked Little Bit."

7

CASSIE FOUND A full skirt and off-the-shoulder blouse to wear with Ian on their musical experience playing in the streets. She couldn't do anything about her short hair, so she decided to simply leave it with a tousled look. She went down to the shop early in the morning, taking her fiddle with her. She spent the morning, between customers, a little nervously, picking at a few things she wanted to do: straightening the merchandise and being sure that each item or basket was price-tagged to make Sarah's first hours in the shop easy.

She was surprised at her feeling of something near reluctance at letting someone else, even someone as pleasant and efficient as Sarah, take over her shop for a few hours. With a mental shrug she accused herself of considering it her baby, and then decided she wasn't feeling any guilt about that. Mentally and physically, Teddy Bear's Christmas Shop had taken her whole concentration since she arrived in San Antonio.

She ate her lunch and then stood at the register and looked at the shop while she waited for Sarah and Ian. It was a shop anyone would be proud to work in, she decided with a warm feeling of pride. Well worth the chances she was taking with her finances.

Sarah and Ian came in together. It was soon obvious that Ian was right. Sarah easily understood the flow of the merchandise set-up and the method of pricing. In the few minutes it took to make her ready to take over the shop, Cassie lost her apprehensions and was ready to enjoy the fun trip with Ian. Sarah, who knew Little Bit well, and had heard the story of his love affair with the bear, just smiled when she saw him on his perch.

Cassie felt a surge of pure happiness, somewhere close to being let out of school, as she went out on the street with Ian. Even so, she was aware that Ian chose to go the other way rather than pass in front of Mitch's shop. She wondered why, since he hadn't hesitated to go by when taking her out to dinner.

She decided to ask him why later. She didn't want to spoil the vibes now.

They followed the River Walk for a while, and then went through a hotel lobby to the street. They crossed the street to wander through Alamo Park and past the Alamo, playing as they went. They spied a young couple, undoubtedly honeymooning, riding in a horse-drawn carriage and followed it, playing their own version of *I Love You Truly*. When they stopped as the carriage made another turn, the young man flipped them a silver dollar. Laughing, they gave it to the first child they met.

They came back to Alamo Park and played for a while for a group of children and their teachers or mothers on an outing, feeling a little like Saint Francis surrounded by little birds, as the babbling children ran in happy circles around them.

Waving good-bye to the mothers who had taken a moment to sit down and relax while the two entertained their children, they went back down to the River Walk, and up to the top of one of the bridges. There they did a playful rendition of *London Bridge Is Falling Down*, while two giggling young girls, forgotten for the moment by their parents, tore a flower and dropped the petals down on the people in a tour boat.

Back down on the River Walk, they played *As Time Goes By* for an older couple sitting at an outdoor café and for two young people walking hand in hand who stopped to listen. With smiling waves, they refused the bill that the older man held out toward them, and drifted on.

They went through the fountain area and back onto the street. Shortly after that, Cassie became aware of a harmonica joining in behind them, harmonizing perfectly with the old Irish tune they were in the midst of. Since Ian went on playing, Cassie did also, thinking this must be someone Ian knew. After Ian had murmured a suggestion of a Western medley, and they were close to the end of it, she felt the harmonica player step in between them.

"I'll just walk along with you," a low voice said. "You just don't stop playing, and don't look at me."

Surprised, Cassie turned to see who was talking, letting her bow drift across the strings into silence.

"I said don't look at me. I said keep playing."

She had time for only a fuzzy outline of a not-too-clean man with whiskers and a pungent odor before the coarsening of his voice told her to do as he said.

"That's a knife against my ribs?" Ian sounded amazingly calm. Cassie thought he hadn't missed a beat on his guitar. She nervously picked up the medley from the beginning again, not playing well.

"Sure is, buddy. Now, which pocket? I don't want people thinking I'm going through all your pockets. Got a watch on worth anything?" The man sounded friendly again.

"Back pocket," Ian told him. "Would you mind taking the driver's license out and putting it back? It's a pain to get it replaced. I don't have a watch."

"Okay." The man was amazingly quick. "Now, lady, let's have yours."

Cassie gulped but tried desperately to keep her voice as casual as theirs were. "Do I look like I can be carrying anything valuable? I'm not wearing a watch, either."

She could sense him looking at her clothes, obviously trying to figure where the pocket holding the paraphernalia any woman would carry could be. "I'm going to pat you down. It's gotta look like I'm just being friendly so don't scream or anything or I'll have to leave my knife hanging from your boyfriend's ribs."

Feeling his left arm around her and his hand running over her body, Cassie got much more of a whiff of his body scent than she wanted. She forced herself to submit to the frustration of having his dirty hand on her person. Thankfully he was quick and there was no lingering that would show any sexual thoughts. The word *professional* went through her mind. Satisfied that she didn't have anything, he dropped his hand.

"Okay. It's always good to do business with people who cooperate."

"Man, you're pretty good with that harmonica," Ian said. "Why don't you get your money that way?"

Cassie wanted to scream at him to shut up and let the man go.

"Ah, sometimes I do. But it's slow coming in. Real slow. How much you take today?"

"Not much. Actually nothing. But we're just playing for fun today."

"Man, I can't afford to do anything for fun. I like to eat."

Ian seemed to insist on not letting the man go. "We have a little group that plays around sometimes. You want to come practice with us?"

"Ian." Cassie put her whole feelings in that name.

"Don't worry, lady. I'm not that innocent. He'd have the cops there."

"Well, if you're feeling daring sometime, come and see." Ian still seemed to be paying no attention to Cassie's alarm.

"Gotta leave you now. There's a bike cop riding over there. Don't they look cute in their little shorts? If you're gonna report me to one of them guys, don't bother. I'm outta here right now."

As suddenly as he had appeared, he was gone. Cassie stopped playing and stood still. "Are you going to report him? We can catch the policeman now."

Ian set the end of his guitar against the sidewalk, looking toward the corner where the thief had disappeared. "No. They'd never catch him. But that policeman helped us just by being there. You know, that guy was pretty good with the harmonica."

"Ian. He took your wallet. All your money. Your cards. Why don't you report him? "

He grinned. "No cards. I don't have any. If he thinks the money in that wallet will get him anywhere he's in for a shock. He put the driver's license back in my pocket. Pretty thoughtful, I'd say. Sometimes these guys get mad when you don't have much of anything to be robbed of. Maybe we can help him go straight and play harmonica in our group sometime."

Cassie shuddered. "Give him a bath first."

He looked thoughtful. "Maybe Nerina knows him," he said, almost to himself.

"Nerina? She knows street people? Muggers?"

Cassie thought he looked surprised that she had heard him. Or sorry, perhaps.

"Nerina is—different, sometimes. He wasn't violent."

"She certainly is." Cassie decided to answer the first part of his statement, leaving a large opening for more information.

But he didn't add anything more. "You want to go back to your shop now?"

"Desperately."

They went back the shortest way, which was past Mitch's shop. Sarah was waiting on a customer when they entered

Teddy Bear's, and she only smiled as Cassie and Ian came in. Ian waved to her, and gave Cassie a brief good-bye before slipping out. The customer was barely out of the shop before Mitch strode in.

"Where's Ian?" he asked, without a greeting to either Cassie or Sarah.

"He went on," Cassie said, putting her fiddle into its case and stashing it behind the register. "I guess he didn't know you wanted to see him."

"I guess he didn't," Mitch growled. "After taking you out playing on the street."

Cassie looked at him, almost too surprised to feel angry. Playing on the street was fun and something a lot of musicians did. What was wrong with him? And how did he think he had the right to question anything she did?

"He didn't 'take' me," she said, making her fingers into quotation marks. "I do what I want to do. And it was fun. Except for the mugger," she added musingly, aware that some little imp inside her was perversely trying to make him more upset.

She succeeded. "The mugger? Ian took you into the street and let someone threaten you? No wonder he didn't want to face me."

Up until now, Cassie had been only mildly wondering what was bugging Mitch. But this was too much. She boiled out from behind the register and stood as tall as possible, feeling as if she was almost looking directly into his eyes.

"Mitch Williams, no one takes me anywhere and I can take care of myself, and nobody has to answer to anyone for what happens to me—" Her voice trailed off as she realized she was standing much too close to him so that her whole body was feeling sensations from his body, and she was acutely aware of some emotion in him that changed those gray-green eyes to something deeper.

"And you can take your cat with you

when you go," she sputtered, trying to push away from her overloaded nerve endings.

Mitch looked up at Little Bit, who was sitting up on the bear's lap watching them with interest. "He's too determined to have his own way," he said. "Like you."

He turned and went out.

"Green, I think," Sarah, who had been leaning on the counter watching them, said thoughtfully.

"Green?"

"The eyes. Definitely green. Today. "

"Control freak."

"Not before now. Not usually. He's jealous."

"Of me? Not with long-legged Nerina wound around him. He can't see past her."

"Oh. Well, that's something else."

Still feeling the rather-violent nerve shock of her sudden nearness to Mitch, Cassie whirled to look at Sarah. "You're the second person to say something like that. What does it mean?"

Sarah rested her hand lightly on Cassie's shoulder. "Perhaps later. We had several lookers and some customers this afternoon. Thanks for letting me look after the shop—along with Little Bit. You didn't really mean for Mitch to take him away, did you? He's your best salesman."

She took the pay that Cassie offered and started to leave. Near the door, she turned back. "Cassie. All of us in the band know that Mitch isn't responding to Nerina. Not in any way that would bother you."

"Bother me?" Cassie sputtered. "Why would anything about them bother me?"

But Sarah had already gone with a final smile and a wave, going by way of Mitch's shop, Cassie was sure.

Cassie looked up at Little Bit. "Actually, I'm almost learning to like you. Not just for your salesmanship. You sit up there raining down comfort and wisdom like a kindly old judge, and I—I can't believe I'm starting to talk to you like a friend. So what do you think about The Witch From the Sea? And why do I care? And I think I'll buy you some nice treats. Okay, so I'm refusing to think about Mitch and his wicked ways. Maybe what Rosie says is true. He just wants to chase me out of here and bring his leggy friend in to dance to the music, no matter what Sarah sees, because that's what she wants to see, and he'll get shelves the first day he's in here, and stools to sit on and listen to the CDs. But you'd better bet that you'll be sorry because I'll take the bear when I go—if I were going, which I'm no way not."

Little Bit jumped down and walked out. "Traitor," Cassie called after him, and then looked around carefully to see that nobody heard her. When she saw Mitch coming toward her door, she went behind a tree and pretended to be carefully moving decorations around. How dare he come back again while she was so angry with him?

He stood just inside the door. "Please come out from behind that tree, Cassie. I want to say I'm sorry. I know that I don't have any right to question what you do. I was just so concerned about you, even if I don't have the right for that, either. I want what's best for you."

"To be back in Dallas, for instance?" she called.

"Of course not back in Dallas. Here in San Antonio. And if you won't come out, I'm coming in there with you."

She moved quickly. "No don't. I'm com—"

She didn't finish the sentence before she slammed into him, their arms somehow fitting together with both their hands curved around the other's elbows, and their mouths seeming to be close to touching. She sensed his hands drawing her closer and his lips moving slightly downward toward hers, as she felt all the anger and suspicion draining out of her mind and knew that her own lips were waiting for his.

As they moved, she realized they were standing much too close to the tree. It swayed gently beside them, the ornaments jingling like a warning bell. They both reached out to catch it. Several minutes of bringing it back to a safe position tore the mood to practicality.

Mitch didn't try to change the mood back, but he looked seriously at her. "Just the same," he said. "Just the same."

He turned and went out.

She stood where he left her for several minutes. What did that mean? Did he ever leave her with any answers?

Anyway, this day surely had made him realize that she was no pushover who would let him and his father shove her out of Teddy Bear's Christmas Shop.

If Rosie was right and that was what they were planning to do.

8

"SARAH AND I are singing at church tomorrow. Come with me?" Mitch caught her on Saturday morning coming out of Rosie's place with coffee and a bagel in her hands. If he was remembering their near-kiss, or had given it any thought at all, he certainly wasn't showing it. He took her coffee while she manipulated the strawberry jam-covered bagel that Rosie had carefully wrapped in an open napkin and unlocked the door to Teddy Bear's Christmas Shop.

Cassie thought for only a moment before agreeing. She was curious about the church that Sarah would choose. Showing Mitch that nothing awful had happened after her street music adventure with Ian would be excellent, too. Also, she could be careful to show him by her attitude that their almost-kiss meant nothing to her, as it seemed to with him, and, she added breathlessly inside her mind, that he had no right to be concerned about her. She tried to stop the thought that it would be a little bit nice to have him concerned about her. She realized that she had failed before she realized that he was talking again.

"Good. I'll pick you up at ten. I'll drive."

Without asking how far it was, Cassie didn't question the time, and a spate of customers kept her from thinking much about the invitation while she worked the shop. There was little question in her mind about what she would wear. She had only one gray business suit that would be suitable.

If she took special care with her looks on this first occasion Mitch would see her in a anything but her work and band practice clothes (and one street music garb, she reminded herself), it was only because they were going to a church, not for his opinion.

He wasn't wearing the expected suit and tie when she slid onto the seat of his sports car. She assumed it was because he would be wearing a choir robe at church. She fought to not dwell on how fine he looked in his well-tailored slacks and close-fitting knit shirt.

Her first sight of the church brought a quick impression that it somehow looked like Sarah. No, like Sarah's personality. Like the church Sarah would choose.

It was small, and some architect could have had a business in mind when he planned it. Or maybe the church couldn't afford anything more than a square brick building set with a small parking lot, between other small brick buildings that boasted business signs. It could easily have been a business building at one time,

Cassie thought, as she walked with Mitch to a side door.

"We'll have coffee in the basement," he explained, guiding her down a series of steps, after she got a glimpse through an open door of a very plain sanctuary. "For the early birds. And Sarah and I need to run through the song one time. She sings here often, and I've sung with her here a few times."

The basement wasn't the gray concrete Cassie expected. The walls had been painted, and murals from Bible stories covered the lower space while fluffy white clouds and a great vivid rainbow floated above.

"They have pre-school in here on weekdays," Mitch said, noticing her delighted expression as she appreciated the joy in the murals.

"Lucky kids," she murmured. "Good artist who did the murals. They must have taken a big slice of the church budget."

A strange expression drifted across his face. Almost uncomfortable, she thought. But he only answered, "It was donated."

She dropped the subject and looked around at the rest of the room. People were walking around or sitting at square tables placed about the room, with plastic coffee cups and cookies that looked homemade in their hands. Cassie smiled a little nervously, aware of interested looks. But she relaxed when she realized that they were smiling and friendly. Most of the men were wearing slacks and open-necked shirts, and the women were equally casually dressed.

"Why didn't you tell me?" she asked in a low tone. "I'm terribly overdressed."

As usual he didn't answer directly. "Some of the older ladies will be dressier when we go upstairs to the sanctuary."

Mentally shrugging since she couldn't change now, Cassie passed up the cookies but accepted coffee. Mitch led her to a table where a young couple with three boys greeted them. He introduced Cassie to Karen and Kenneth Morris, explaining to the couple that she had a new shop next to his on the River Walk. The conversation was open, and the three children were a part of it. Obviously Mitch came there often enough that he was well-known.

Karen quickly told them that they came early in order to hear Sarah and Mitch practice. "That way," she said, smiling, "we get to hear them twice."

While they waited for Sarah to arrive, Karen explained that she had chosen to home-school the children, and amused them with some stories of her early attempts to get the tutoring under way.

"I have to admit," Kenneth said, "that at first I wasn't very helpful. Karen is a creative person. She has always made great pottery, but I was almost convinced that she wasn't down to earth enough to teach the boys. Now I realize that it's the creativity that makes her home schooling successful. And somewhere there she finds time to still make great pottery."

"We've got it all together now," Karen said easily.

The boys all nodded enthusiastically.

"We went to the Witte museum yesterday," the oldest one said. "It's really neat. We played with a lot of things there, and I liked the tree house. And we don't have to sit as long as the kids in regular school. But," he added with a hint of wistfulness, "I miss the kids sometimes."

"We're getting a larger group together for trips and playing," Karen explained, just before Sarah came in.

Sarah looked stressed for time, carrying a guitar carelessly in one hand. A well-scrubbed Danny came in behind her, wearing pressed jeans and a white T-shirt. Danny immediately took several cookies and went to a table on the other side of the room. After a quick question to his mother, the oldest Morris boy went to join them.

Sarah and Mitch talked a minute while the conversation stopped and the people in the room sat back to listen to them. Sarah accompanied on the guitar as the two blended their voices. Cassie was amiably surprised that they sang a pleasing rendition of *Away in a Manger*, and then did a special arrangement of *Jesus Loves Me*.

"We're having a special assembly for the children today," Karen explained in a low voice.

After they had run through the songs once, Keith Thomas came in. Looking sleepy but amiable as usual, he took the guitar from Sarah, backing them for the next run-through.

Then everyone stood to go up the stairs to the sanctuary in a happy jumble. Cassie sat for church with the Morris family, feeling a satisfying aura of spirituality in the bare little sanctuary. It was only increased by the enthusiasm for the absolutely awful, special-for-this-service children's choir, and the simple homily the minister delivered designed for the children.

Mitch and Sarah sang with the accompaniment of Keith's guitar to enthusiastic applause. After the service, Mitch met her when she came out of the pew and kept a soft pressure on her back with his left hand as he responded to the appreciation of the other people moving toward the door. The pressure didn't ease when they had negotiated the sidewalk and moved away from the rapidly dispersing congregation.

"Every time I look at the leaves still on the trees I wonder if it really is almost Christmas," Cassie said, looking around as they walked across the parking lot.

"I'm taking you to lunch, you know."

"No I don't think you mentioned that before."

"I know. If I gave you time to think about it you would probably remember a really good reason why you can't. Sarah will mind your shop this afternoon if you agree. My dad will watch mine."

She stopped and faced him, ignoring the stares of the other churchgoers who walked around them.

"Maybe we should celebrate. Do you know what you just did? No, I don't mean for you to reply. Because I'm sure you can't do it twice. You made a remark to me that had some connection to what I had just said. I've been thinking that you never hear me."

"Really? Well, later we lose the leaves for a short time. Just so new ones can grow on."

After a short mental fight about paying out money to Sarah from Teddy Bear's tiny net receipts, compared to a full afternoon off, compared to a sandwich in her apartment, compared to a fuller meal than she'd had recently, compared to giving up and spending that afternoon with Mitch, compared to getting closer to finding out what his real goal was—she agreed. "All right. It looks like it's already planned. Are we going back to the river for lunch?"

He signaled an okay to Sarah, who gave Cassie a friendly wave. "We're catching that trolley. I'll leave my car here."

"The trolley that just went by?"

"No, that wasn't the one we want. The one coming. We can beat it to the stop."

It was obvious that he had also planned wherever this lunch was to be. She wondered if it was to be at an upscale restaurant, remembering Rosie's comments about Mitch's family.

The trolley gave an impression of an interesting old square machine that somehow moved on its own without the help of anything like a modern engine. Red-painted railings and plastic seats contrasted with brass poles. Two men stood in a railed deck on the back talking, though there were several empty seats inside.

There was little time for talking inside the trolley as Cassie held tightly onto the edge of her seat to keep the sudden sharp turns from pushing her against Mitch. She looked out the window, refusing to meet his eyes, but she was irritatingly aware that he was thoroughly enjoying her desperate attempts to keep a distance between them and her uncontrolled quick breaths when he slipped one arm around her, tucking her closely enough that she could feel ribs under his lean side.

Lunch was at a surprisingly simple café where Sunday breakfast was still being served, and Mitch seemed to know the young waiter. He suggested a meat-and-three lunch and she found it delicious, so much better than the cheese sandwiches and peanut butter toast that she had subsisted on much too often lately.

After lunch Mitch kept them standing a few moments outside on the street corner.

"I want to show you something. It's not far. We can walk."

"Is it another of San Antonio's interesting historical sites?"

"Danny won't be there now. His mom cooks a marvelous Sunday meal. She invited us, but I told her another time."

She shrugged, accepting another of his no-answer answers, and fell in beside him. She soon found herself fascinated by the neighborhood as they walked through an old area of small houses where several people working in tiny yards waved to them. Enough blocks later that she was beginning to feel the effects of wearing higher heels rather than her usual work flats, he turned off the sidewalk abruptly and led her down a grass-covered lane. She noticed that the lane had been kept well-mowed, more curious than ever about where it might lead.

"Here we are." He opened an old wrought-iron gate so overflowing with twisted forms that it almost seemed to have figures clinging to it. Cassie wanted to stop and investigate it, but his hand on her back gently pushed her past it and into an ancient cemetery surrounded by pointed posts connecting a wrought-iron fence.

"It's over here," he said, "just past that tall monument."

Cassie followed him quietly. Where was he taking her? To the grave of someone well known? His family? No, his family was in the East. Perhaps something to do with his interest in the history of San Antonio?

He stopped beside a simple concrete form, child-sized, surrounded by monuments of different ages. A spray of cheap plastic flowers lay at the head.

"This is where Sarah's family has been buried for generations." He indicated the tiny grave. "Your angel," he said.

"Angel? I don't see an angel."

"Danny is a child of this world."

Cassie looked at him, letting her

lack of understanding show. He went on before she could say anything, and she realized that he was just finishing a thought.

"He knows that some people are willing to steal from the dead. Look under the flowers."

Intrigued, Cassie slipped to her knees, ignoring the feel of grass on her nylon-covered legs, and gently lifted the flowers. The ceramic angel knelt there. For an emotional moment she almost thought she and the angel were doing a mirror imitation of each other's positions. She felt something spearing into her mind: an unexpected knowledge of the artist's passion—something from Danny's feelings—she couldn't identify the fleeting impressions. She seemed to be coming back from some other world when she became aware of Mitch talking to her.

"Danny's little sister died two years ago. Just a few months old. His father couldn't take it. He left soon after, and no one knows where he is. Danny wanted her to have the angel ornament because she never got to see one on a Christmas tree."

Cassie looked down at the angel, wanting to hide the tears that rushed to her eyes. Danny was willing to give up his skates to be able to place this angel on his sister's grave. Mitch gave her some time to herself, and she felt for a moment that only she and the angel and Danny's little sister were in the cemetery. Then he caught her by the waist and lifted her to her feet.

She felt that she had to return to the practical world. "Do you think he may have had other reasons than just wanting to give her the angel?" she asked, not looking at Mitch. "I'm not a psychologist, but I've read that children sometimes need to make up for—for something they may think they've done to cause the death or the father leaving."

He didn't remove his hands from her

waist. "I don't know, Cassie. I'm not a psychologist, either. But I wanted you to know why it was so important for Danny to have the angel. I saw your face while I was paying you for it. The youth minister at the church is staying close to Danny. The one you saw today."

Cassie felt certain that the man whose homily she had so thoroughly enjoyed earlier could support Danny. Wanting to lean against Mitch for a long, long time without talking, she instead moved away from his hands, aware that they fell emptily to his sides but rejecting any more intimacy with him. She led the way out of the cemetery, keeping as much distance between them as possible.

They walked to catch the trolley in near-silence, broken occasionally by a low-voiced comment on something one of them saw.

"Let's go on the River Walk," Mitch said after they had picked up his car and he had parked it in a garage a few blocks from their shops, the same one where she kept her own little Bug. "Let's just be tourists. It's too great a day to waste. Later, I'll make you sandwiches, and we'll have an evening picnic over by the Alamo."

Ready to move away from the emotions of the cemetery, but not ready to see Sarah just yet, Cassie didn't argue with his taking it for granted that she would follow his wishes, as she might have done earlier. She let him lead the way, agreeing with her silence. A silence that lasted comfortably while they went down to the River Walk and wandered with a strolling crowd through its meanderings, enjoying the nature about them in the gentle movements of the treetops and bushes beside the river, as well as the boatloads of laughing people on the river.

They were almost forced by the number of people on the sidewalk to walk breathtakingly close, occasionally moving away from each other to let oncoming strollers go between them, and then coming back together, as though following the steps of some phantom dance. She noticed several young couples holding hands as they walked. She sternly refused to allow herself to accept a desire to feel her hand folded into his. No way did she ever want even something like the cemetery experience make her get closer to him. She let Rosie's frequent words came back to her like a mantra, pushing her to be only close enough to him to watch him carefully.

Having put herself securely at a mental distance from him, she let him lead her past spring water flowing over man-made concrete steps. They came out across the street from the Alamo Plaza. Mitch indicated one of several raised concrete seats, and she sat down beside him.

Even though people moved back and forth in front of them, laughter drifted to them, and cars passed in the street, Cassie's sense of the true spirit of the

Alamo came through more intensely sitting there than it had when she had been inside the building.

She felt a silence that clung to the grounds and the simple building, under the ongoing sounds of visitors. A silence that brought her the spirits, not only of the men who died there, but also of the actions, the emotions, the fears and determination—not just of the Texans, but also of the simple Mexicans who fought with General Santa Ana. She was oddly aware of Santa Ana's anger that someone dared to resist him, of those men with him who knew that, even if there would be a final victory, some of them would die achieving it, and that they would kill other men.

"They came from this direction, from across the river," she murmured, setting the scene in her mind, almost forgetting that Mitch was there, and then being grateful that he could allow her this time without asking that she explain herself.

After a while they crossed the street to the Plaza grounds. Cassie sat on a bench to wait while Mitch went across to make the sandwiches. She watched a man in a wheelchair who seemed to be alone, and a small boy in a Davy Crockett fur hat guarding the Alamo with a flintlock gun held up on his shoulder while his mother took pictures. They fit into the mood from the church, Danny's angel, and her heightened senses here by the Alamo.

Sitting there she remembered that this was the same bench on the same Plaza where she had sat another Sunday afternoon, with the same, or one nearly like the same, band playing the same South American music. But, she realized, today is changed. Today is it's own, moved away from any battles about the shops. She could almost pretend that there was nothing before today in San Antonio, or anything to follow. Almost.

Then she smiled quietly to herself, watching Mitch carrying a red ice chest.

"Thanks, Little Bit," she said. "Or maybe not." A memory of Rosie's warning about Mitch's real goals jerked her out of the gentle aura. She forced herself back to her need to keep a wary attitude toward him.

"What did you say? Sorry I missed it." Mitch put the chest on the grass and sat down beside her before he leaned over to bring out two wrapped sandwiches and a bag of potato chips. He opened a Thermos of iced tea and poured two paper cups dangerously full. Cassie searched carefully for an even spot in the grass to set her cup down, giving herself time to consider that it was best that she stay away from dreamy moods, to be alert to the possibility of being played for a fool by this man.

"Just that you've fed me three times now and I'll do the same for you sometime," she said. "I make a great peanut butter and cracker sandwich."

The sandwiches were a combination

of meat and greens. They ate and watched couples, families, and loners with dogs, in a silence that was as comfortable as if they had discussed earlier that they both liked people watching.

She reluctantly went with him back to their separate shops, but Sarah's report of a good afternoon's sales was a great ending to the day. Remembering the visit to the baby's grave, she hesitated on the brink of mentioning it to Sarah but, looking at her expression, she knew that Sarah had known where they were going when they left the church parking lot, eons earlier in the day.

Wondering what would be the best way to start the conversation, Cassie simply let her emotions lead her. Without any planning, she and Sarah hugged, and then stepped back with tears in their eyes.

"You understand about Danny." It wasn't a question, and Cassie only nodded. With another short hug, Sarah left.

Cassie undressed for bed that evening, trying not to let her mind dissect the up-and-down, push-and-pull of the day. To get away from emotions she didn't want to handle, she sat down at what she laughingly called her dining table, though she mostly used it as a computer table, and flicked open her e-mail. Intermingled with business messages she didn't want to contend with, she found one from her mother.

Cassie, Dear
I'll be there for sure on Wednesday. I can stay through Christmas. Anything I can help with in the shop? See you Wednesday.

9

CASSIE READ HER mother's message with a surge of delight. She'd missed being in the same town as her mother even though she hadn't lived with her since college. But she had worked in her mother's Christmas Shop in Dallas since junior high, and had helped manage it since her father died. She'd learned all her marketing smarts there. Julia Rogers was a genius at displaying wares. Cassie expected a lot of advice and moving about of merchandise, some of which she would accept.

She was right. Julia arrived shortly after lunch, let Cassie take her two small pieces of luggage upstairs, went to Rosie's shop for coffee, and then announced that she was bright as a penny and ready for any help that Cassie might need.

Cassie hugged her again. "Mom, I am looking forward to your ideas about display. They're always good. But now just sit down and talk to me. I've missed you."

Julia returned the hug with a series of happy squeezes. She stepped back, then forward to hug Cassie again. "Oh, missing—you've no idea about missing until your very favorite and only daughter moves out of town. But I'm swollen with pride about what you're doing down here in San Antone."

Cassie grinned. "You almost sang that, Mom. I could hear guitars and fiddles playing behind your melody of *Old San Antone*."

Julia returned her grin. "Speaking of music, look me in the eyes, which happen to have always been on an exact level with yours, showing what a genius I am in creating the perfect daughter, and tell me about this group you got into in such a hurry."

"Yeah, Mom, and the eyes are still the same color as mine, but somehow the hair isn't. You've been experimenting with Clairol, haven't you?"

"Well, not exactly doing it on my own, but since I must now cover a gray hair or two, I thought I might as well have some fun with it. It's called champagne number never you mind."

"It looks good. I'm not sure it doesn't make you look younger then me, though."

"Don't try to con me, girl. I'm still older and wiser." Julia went silent for a moment, noticing for the first time the makeshift stairway for Little Bit's climb to the bear's lap. She went over and stood before it with hands on her hips, in an exaggerated physical demonstration of disbelief.

After letting enough time go by that Cassie had to understand her opinion,

Julia turned to face her feckless daughter. "So tell me what this is. You've got so much room you can afford unused space?"

"It's for Little Bit." Cassie carefully kept her mouth from twitching into a grin. "Remember, I told you about the cat from the bookstore next door? Owen Williams had me move that Christmas tree display over to the other side of the door, and then had the two shelves put in so Little Bit can jump to the bear's lap without breaking anything. It's really working well."

Julia didn't look persuaded. "Owen Williams? He owns the cat?"

"Mitch Williams owns the cat. Owen Williams is his father. He's visiting from the East. They have a string of book and music stores there. I'm sure you'll meet him."

Julia frowned. Cassie could read her expression. Already she didn't like the father of Mitch Williams, who came into her daughter's shop and rearranged it. If anyone was going to do that, the mother of Cassie Rogers was here now to take care of it.

Cassie laughed and hugged her mother one more time. "It's so good to see you, Mom. But I'm starting to like Little Bit. He's making the shop famous by word of mouth. People bring their kids in to see him sleeping in the bear's lap. This is the kind of marketing you'd think up. Come see the rest of the shop."

Julia looked back at the Little Bit set-up as they moved away. "Just the same, I can find some way to use more of that space," she said, more to herself than to Cassie.

"Why aren't you using this tree?" she asked, as they moved past the trees glittering with ornaments and bells, to the naked one back by the workroom.

"It's for the little dolls. They're marvelous, Mom. Tiny, but dressed in perfectly made costumes. At least they look that way in the catalog."

"They are that good. I've seen them."

"Well, that's more than I can say. My order seems to keep getting lost." Cassie felt as forlorn as the tree, remembering her daily disappointment when the doll order didn't come.

Before her mother could reply, the phone on the counter rang. Cassie picked it up to find Owen Williams on the line. After talking for a few minutes, she turned to her mother. "Mom, you too tired to go out to dinner this evening? Owen Williams is inviting us. I can fix up something here if you don't want to go. But it won't be as good as his choice."

Cassie was sure she saw a real flame jump to life in Julia's eyes. "How did Owen Williams know I'm here?"

Cassie sighed, holding her hand over the phone. "I think there's something in the air that blocks people from answering questions. He's just next door. He probably saw you. He probably walked by. Do you want to go out to eat?"

Julia Rogers nodded vigorously. "You just bet your life I want to go out with Mister Owen Williams. I've got a few bones to pick with him. A few things to say about his interference in your shop."

Cassie was groaning inwardly all the time she was agreeing to a time for dinner, hearing that Owen would pick them up at the shop, and wondering how much of an event this dinner was going to be. Her mother was already throwing out vibes about Owen Williams, and she hadn't even met him yet. As she hung up the phone, Cassie wondered if Mitch was going to be eating with them, and if she could conceivably come down with a disabling disease between now and then.

Mitch did come with his father to pick them up when both shops closed. Cassie thought thankfully that her mother was reasonably gracious when she introduced the two men. It turned out to be a low-key excursion: a short stroll down the River Walk to one of the outdoor restaurants.

At least she could see that Owen Williams had planned a low-key evening. Julia Rogers hadn't.

"You're from Yankee land?" Julia asked as soon as they were seated at a table beside the River Walk.

Owen's smile was genial. "Connecticut."

Julia seemed to read it as condescending. She attacked as if she wished for a Confederate flag. "You Yankees invading the South again?"

Owen looked bewildered. "We're testing the market in San Antonio. I thought Texas was a Western state."

"You've been seeing too many old cowboy movies." Julia picked up her menu. She spread it in front of her face, seeming to end the conversation.

Feeling sorry for Owen, and wishing she could make her mother stand in a corner until she learned better manners, Cassie took the occasion to open up a conversation about old movies in general and especially Westerns, finding that Mitch and his dad were both fans.

Since the waiter was there to take their orders, Julia had to come out of her cave and admit she was with them. Sometime during the dinner, Cassie managed to make the point that Texas was both Southern and Western, but mostly Western. Mitch followed her lead with a few remarks about the early settlement of the area they were in.

After the meal, which had only a thin skin of sociability spread over it, even though Julia skimmed short of actual rudeness, they parted at their shop doors.

"Mom," Cassie said, fitting her key in the door, "why were you so impolite to Owen Williams? I don't think he could figure you out. And," she added, twisting the key with more vigor than usual, "you know very well, you don't think of yourself as an 'I'll never forget the Uncivil War Southerner.' You're just a proud Texan."

"Impolite?" Julia said, ignoring the comment about the Southerner. "I wasn't impolite. I was on guard. He's an enemy."

"Why? You don't even know him yet."

"I talked to Rosie this afternoon when I went over for coffee."

Cassie, wishing that Rosie wouldn't gossip so quickly with Julia, decided that she didn't want to talk about any of them tonight. She included Rosie, the Williams, father and son, the cat, and possibly her mother. Tomorrow would be soon enough for the conversation Julia seemed to be determined on. She clicked the lock and opened the door.

She stepped inside and stopped in shock.

"Oh, Cassie!" Julia said, putting both hands on Cassie's shoulders. "What a disaster. Turn on the big light."

The shop looked worse in the brighter light. Cassie's logo, the big Teddy Bear, lay face down in front of the shelves that Owen had put up, looking like a flaccid dead body. The top one of the two shelves that Little Bit used to climb up was leaning away from its stand. The statuettes that had stood on the shelf ends were on the floor. One was broken.

"Oh, Teddy Bear, what happened?" Cassie tried to rush toward the bear, but Julia's hands tightened on her shoulders.

"Wait, Cassie. Don't touch it. That bear didn't get down there by itself. And, look, there's ornaments knocked off some of the trees. I wondered why Owen Williams was so fast to invite us out. I told you he's the enemy. Someone came in here while we were out being dined. The place is trashed. Stand still. They may still be here."

"Mom, you've been reading too many mystery novels. I can't believe Owen Williams would do anything like this." Even as she tried to make her mother feel more secure on her first night on the River Walk, Cassie was aware of her own doubts. There was definitely a mess in the shop. They had definitely been lured out, and the mess had definitely happened while they were gone.

Cassie did a visual check while letting her mother hold her still for the moment. The only damage seemed to be right at the bear's location. Surely if someone was intent on trashing the shop they could do a better job than that.

Pleased with her own detective way of thinking, she shrugged off her mother's hands and went over to lift the bear up, examining it carefully. "He hasn't been damaged, thank goodness. Little Bit might not like the smell of a different bear." She stood up at a sudden thought, holding the bear like a baby. "Little Bit. Did we lock him in here when we left?"

She put the bear back down on the floor and went to the counter for a flashlight and shone it around the Christmas trees, calling the cat's name. Just then the phone rang.

"Little Bit's gone," Mitch said. "Is he over there?"

"Well, somebody's been over here." She realized that her voice held a lot of the same tone her mother had used earlier, and she didn't try to change it. Maybe there was something to Julia Rogers's theory. Mitch certainly hadn't taken long to call. Had he expected something to happen in her shop? "Teddy Bear's fallen off his shelf. And there's ornaments on the floor," she added.

"I'll be right over." The phone went dead.

In minutes, Mitch and Owen came in, Mitch carrying his own flashlight. A half-hysterical thought ran through Cassie's mind that they must look like elves at the North Pole who had lost a toy as they all walked around bent over and shining their lights under the trees. If they did, whoever saw them would have to see that they were way far from happy-buddy elves. Julia, especially, walked about as far as possible from the men, with a "humph" expression on her face.

They found Little Bit hiding under one of the smaller Christmas trees. After Mitch spent several minutes asking him gently to come out, he did, and allowed Mitch to pick him up.

While Mitch comforted Little Bit, Owen helped the women check the shop to be sure no one was in there. "I'll call the police if you want," he said.

In spite of her mother's expression, Cassie shook her head, refusing to allow herself to voice her frequently changing opinion that Little Bit was a) a curse or b) a blessing, depending on whether she was ringing up sales or clearing up some kind of chaos.

"There's no sign that anyone broke in, and nothing's actually been damaged. Little Bit just panicked when he found he couldn't get out and messed things up. Someone may have made a noise outside that scared him."

"Just the same, there's something going on there," her mother said when the men were gone, taking a complaining Little Bit with them. "Owen Williams has something to do with this."

"Mom." Cassie determined to keep the conversation light. "You'd think that you and Owen Williams were the Hatfields and McCoys, the way you're acting."

Julia finally allowed herself a weak chuckle. "Just the same, I'm going to watch them for you. I think Rosie's right. That's why he's down here. To push you out. You know they would have taken this space if I hadn't had that contact and found out it was available before it went public."

Cassie refrained from voicing her own suspicions of the men to her mother. It wouldn't help at this point to add to Julia's hostility with her own suspicions about Mitch's real reasons for his friendliness.

Her last thoughts as she curled up on the couch in her apartment, so her mother could have the bed, was that the Christmas season coming up didn't show much possibility of joy and peace. Especially peace.

She woke the next morning to small sounds coming from the shop downstairs. She lay still for a moment, remembering that she was sure she had closed the door to the stairway when they came up the night before. Maybe Julia was right and somebody besides Little Bit had been trashing the shop. Had someone hidden there all night ready to cut their throats if necessary?

She slammed her feet out of bed, catching a toe on a trailing edge of the sheet she'd slept under and hip-hopping across the room in a sort of trying-to-stay-upright dance.

Rubbing her painful toe briefly, she slipped out of her sleep tee and pulled on the first shorts and top she laid her hands

on, clothes that she had moved out from
what was now the guest room and folded
onto a chair, hidden between the refrigerator and wall. She didn't take the time
to notice if they matched colors or think
that she had pulled on a soft cotton T-
shirt instead of the white buttoned shirt
she considered her shop uniform.

She looked toward the closed bedroom door and then decided not to dis-
turb Julia, who might grab a hammer
and rush off toward the bookstore next
door. That thought made her hurry back
to her small kitchen to find a weapon of
her own, just in case. Nothing came to
hand except one iron skillet. She would
look like the feisty housewife chasing the
bad guy in an old comedy, but better that
than chasing the bad guy with nothing.
She touched the skillet, thought briefly of
calling nine-one-one, saw a mental vision
of customers being scared away from this
part of the River Walk, and closed her
hand about the skillet handle.

Trying to walk quietly on the uncarpeted stairs, she hurried down to stop at the bottom landing, where the door was open. Listening without breathing, she didn't hear anything. Whoever was hiding had stopped moving. Carefully and silently she moved one foot onto the faint stain from the earlier basin overflow. Every suspicious thought about Mitch Williams came bubbling into her mind at the memory. Dropping all thought of sensible restraint, she plunged the other foot down, moving swiftly into the shop, ready to enjoy slamming the skillet across someone's thick skull.

"That you, Cassie?" Julia called from somewhere in the front of the shop.

"Mom!" Cassie took in a deep breath and forcibly stopped her advance with a hand against the register counter. "What? I thought—why are you down here so early? You couldn't have had breakfast without waking me."

Julia came around a tree, her hands

full of fluffy bears. "I have to get started early. How long is it now till Christmas?"

"You know."

"Right. You've got exactly five days to get all the custom you'll get before the after-Christmas markdowns. I got coffee and croissants next door." She stared at Cassie. "Why are you carrying that skillet?"

"I heard someone down here, and I didn't know who it might be," Cassie said, letting a sliver of irony color her voice. "Did you happen to notice the sky and the river while you were out?"

"I was busy carrying my coffee. That Rosie is a smart one. She's caught on to every little plot the Williamses have." Julia walked toward the door. "That monster of a cat is out there."

"So's Mitch," Cassie said. "Never mind, Mom," she added, as her mother turned her back to the door, glaring. "I'll get the door."

"You're letting him in?"

"If you'd come out of hiding there, you'd see that he's carrying a pretty heavy ladder." And, some part of her noticed, dressed in a tight T-shirt and jeans. He must have dressed as hastily as she had. "To put the bear back up, I would guess," she added rapidly, not allowing herself to respond to any show of well-built muscles as he waited for her to let him in.

Mitch untangled his feet from Little Bit's rush through the door and put the tall stepladder down with a sigh that turned into a low sound of appreciation of Cassie's unorthodox attire. After a moment of letting his reaction show openly in his eyes, he seemed to force his gaze to her hands. This was followed by a quickly suppressed grin.

"Did I interrupt breakfast?"

Cassie looked down at her right hand, still clutching the black skillet. She kept her expression bland and her body stiffly dignified as she silently carried the skillet over to the table in her workroom, perfectly aware of his concentration on her back in the well-fitting shorts and top. She stayed in the workroom for a few minutes, letting her lungs remember how to breathe naturally. Of course the breathlessness was still from the scare her mother had given her. She took one deep breath and went back out to the shop.

Mitch was now staring at Little Bit's damage. "He must have been really shook up to have caused so much damage coming down," he said, looking at the leaning step. "Though the men didn't put up anything very solid with those steps."

Little Bit followed him over to the steps, took one look at the bear sprawled on the floor, and ran for his hideaway under a tree.

"Cats do have a memory," Cassie mused. "He may not want to climb up there again."

"Good." Julia nodded. "We'll let the shelves stay, but I'll cover them with scenes of the gnomes over there."

"It's the cat that people come in to visit," Cassie insisted. "And then buy something. You'll see."

"I'll see." Julia's expression and her emphasis on the word told Cassie that she would say a great deal more if Mitch weren't there acting like (pretending to be?) a good neighbor.

Mitch moved Little Bit's steps away from their place. "I'm pretty sure they wouldn't hold me," he commented.

He concentrated on working the metal stepladder into the little space beside Teddy Bear's shelf. He gathered up the bear, carried it up, and positioned it firmly on its high shelf, then stepped down to set the lower shelves back in place.

"I think he'll go back up. Little Bit has a mighty strong hankering for that bear."

As though he intended for his words to show a deeper meaning, his gaze went back to Cassie. Julia's expression showed that she noticed. Cassie thought she saw a

mental target, circled in bright red, flying
from Julia eyes to Mitch's chest. Perhaps
it was time for her to explain to Julia that
she was also wary of Mitch's real deep-
down intentions.

"Thank you, Mitch," she said, being
careful not to look as if she had understood any message he might have been
sending. She was also careful not to let
any unwelcome remnant of such a message settle into her own mind.

"We're spending a good deal of time
repairing Little Bit's ravages over here,"
he said, freeing her from having to call
him a good neighbor, a name she couldn't
truthfully use. Not without Rosie's
inspired gossip anyway.

He took the ladder back to his shop
without trying to get Little Bit to come
out and use his steps again. Cassie and
her mother went about neatening the
merchandise without paying attention to the cat. After an hour of moping
under the tree, Little Bit ventured out

of his retreat, hunkered down with his paws tucked under him while he looked around, and then jumped back up to his love as though nothing frightening had ever happened.

Cassie compromised with Julia by getting her interested in marketing changes in the rest of the shop, but it remained obvious that Julia and Little Bit would never be friends. Cassie suspected that went for Little Bit's owners, too.

She was glad when Ian Weaver came in. After meeting her mother and helping Cassie explain the pick-up band, he left when a couple of customers came in. Julia waited until the women had chosen several small decorations before she commented on Ian, but Cassie made a small bet with herself that the comment would be good when it came.

She was right. "Now there's a nice young man."

"He is," Cassie answered. "He's a good friend already."

"Good friend!" Julia flipped her hand in the air. "He's just ready to be a whole lot more than that, I can tell."

Cassie decided that another subject she wasn't ready to discuss was Ian and the tangled emotions toward The Siren From the Sea. And, of course, Mitch.

10

"YOU REALIZE THAT if Rosie should close, we would simply starve," Julia told Cassie as she brought in a birthday breakfast of coffee and sweet rolls. "But, breakfast is just the start today. I have a surprise to make up for giving birth to you so close to Christmas."

Cassie cleared a space for the unhealthy breakfast beside the cash register and helped Julia unload.

"Mom, thanks, but I don't get mad about that anymore. I grew up."

Julia leaned against the counter, crossing her still slender, pant-clad legs at the ankle. "Just the same. I repeat. I have a birthday surprise."

Cassie grinned, taking a mouthful of

pecan-smothered sweetness. "Ummm, you remember my favorite flavor in all the world next to chocolate." She luxuriated in a long, slow swallow before she considered her mother's surprise, knowing from experiences since childhood that it would be something unique to Julia's creative mind. "So long as it doesn't require time out from the shop. It's getting too close to Christmas to leave now."

"Well, actually it does require that. We're going to be day tourists in San Antonio." Julia held up both hands as Cassie started to protest. "No problem. I called Ian because I figured he would know available people, and he did. Your friend, Sarah, is coming in to mind the store, and paying her is part of my surprise."

"Mom, you could just say Happy Birthday, but, okay, it's going to be good to go out seeing some of the rest of San Antonio with you. What's up?"

Julia spread her hands wide. "El Mercado. And you shall pick out something Mexican and beautiful, and that will be my birthday present to you. Something for your pitifully plain apartment, not for the shop."

Cassie stifled a smile. Julia Rogers was the shopping person. She would undoubtedly find more things she wanted than Cassie would. But the idea of spending an afternoon with her mother in the Mercado, where authentic Mexican art pieces were side by side with jumbles of touristy creations, appealed to her.

Sarah came in mid-morning and, after an introduction that showed an immediate rapport between the two older women, Cassie and Julia caught a trolley to Market Square. They were feeling so celebratory about spending an afternoon together that they laughed when they realized that they had caught the trolley on the wrong side of the street and had circled back to their original stop before actually going toward Market Square. Every time the short turns threw them against each other they started laughing again. Cassie thought of the Sunday trip with Mitch but decided not to spoil the mood by mentioning it to her mother. Instead she enjoyed Julia's fascination with the colorful old trolley. Three young pre-teens prattled on the railed platform at the back, under the watchful eyes of their parents.

Their happiness stayed with them while they got off the trolley at the Market, and found a colorful restaurant. They ordered the hottest of beef and chicken tamales with guacamole and sauces they didn't recognize but dared each other to try.

Three wandering musicians with old guitars and great voices came in while they were eating. After they listened to an energetic Mexican piece, Julia beckoned the musicians over to their table. She slipped some bills to them and asked them to sing *La Paloma*, whispering something to them when they finished. The three men circled behind Cassie and sang the *Happy Birthday* song while a waiter brought her a sweet confection with a candle stuck in it.

"Mom," Cassie protested, "that's for children."

"So. You are my child. Enjoy that stack of calories, whatever it is."

"Help me." Cassie handed her a spoon, and they ate the sweetly delicious stuff together.

Later, Cassie grinned to herself, thinking how right she was about the shopping. Julia was still enthusiastically winding from one market space to another long after she, herself, was growing less and less interested in the souvenir statues and even the better art. Soon after they started, she had marked an imaginative dragon as her choice for the apartment, and when Julia finally filled her arms with purchases, they went back to pick it up.

"I'm sorry we have to leave so early," Julia said after they had settled their packages into the return trolley, "but you're being given a surprise party this evening."

"A surprise party? You're telling me now?"

Julia grinned at her. "Well, aren't you surprised?"

Cassie thought for a minute. "It's frightening, but I think I may be following your train of thought. Am I supposed to act surprised when it happens?"

Julia shook her head, catching a round package that kept threatening to slip off her lap every time the trolley turned. "Not really. Just don't expect it in the shop. And let's talk about something else now. Like what a good sport I am to let our evil neighbors be a part of the party."

"So long as it isn't at the O.K."

"At the O.K.?"

"O.K. Corral. Texas shoot-out. You and the evil neighbors."

"Where's your history, girl? That was Oklahoma. Or was it Kansas? Anyway, we get out here."

Sarah gave Cassie only a secretive smile after Julia paid her and she was ready to leave. Cassie thought of telling her that Julia couldn't keep a secret and she knew about the surprise party, but just let herself enjoy Sarah's enjoyment of looking forward to the party. Everything about Sarah was a pleasure.

Julia sent her daughter up to the apartment with instructions to dress. "Wear that colorful skirt and blouse I saw hanging in your closet," she instructed. "It isn't going to be cold tonight."

Cassie recognized the description of the skirt and off-shoulder blouse she wore to do street music with Ian. She wouldn't mind if that should be the plan for tonight, she mused as she slipped the clothes on.

When she came back down, Mitch was there with cups of chai, that wonderful drink of boiled tea and milk that he had brought from an Indian restaurant farther down the River Walk. His first expression was of intense delight as he looked at her. Then she saw it change and knew with an inward giggle that he was lost in his memory of that day Ian had taken her out on the street.

"For your birthday," he said, managing to put on a pretense of not remembering. "Can you come outside to drink it?"

Julia frowned, but waved Cassie away. "I'll watch here," she said.

"She just wants to get me out so she can move things around the way she thinks they should be," Cassie commented as they settled down on what Cassie was beginning to think of as their bench. "How do you like my outfit?" she asked mischievously, reveling in her ability to tease him for once. He was so good at annoying her. "Mom told me to wear it. She told me about the surprise party, too."

Mitch apparently chose to not rise to her bait. "I planned a celebration of the fact that you were born just for us, but you're too popular." Mitch's frown was eased by a quirky upward twist of his mouth that made it seem very interesting to Cassie. An unacceptable thought of how it would feel to press her finger—or her mouth—to that upward tilted corner slipped quickly through her mind.

She hurriedly turned her gaze from his mouth to the river. Then, moving slightly away from him, she turned to watch a probably retired couple stop to look into her shop where Julia was restyling groups of merchandise between slow sales. Being careful not to sigh as the couple decided not to go in, Cassie turned back to him.

"Mom hasn't even asked me to pretend to be surprised tonight. What kind of a surprise is that?"

She wasn't really asking a question. She could pretend surprise or not, whichever they wanted, though her first choice might be to keep the shop open and bring in some money—a subject that sometimes kept her from sleeping at night. It was getting so close to Christmas and not enough of that commodity was coming in. Perhaps she had been unwise to open the shop at this time, but if she hadn't taken it when it was offered someone else would have. Mitch Williams, if Rosie's gossip was correct

"The surprise is where the party is to be." That mouth stretched into a full mesmerizing grin now.

"And you aren't going to tell me, are you?"

He took a sip of chai and let it rest in his mouth for a moment before swallowing it, a nasty twinkle in his eyes. It seemed to her that they turned more green than gray when he was suppressing some knowledge or emotion.

"Well, if you think that I'm going to beg, you're way wrong." She enjoyed a sip of her own drink, pretending not to be aware of any part of his face, even though it seemed to be moving closer to her own. That mouth only inches away from hers.

"Oh, no, I don't think you're going to beg for that." Again that grins.

"Well, what else would I beg you for?"

"Oh." He pretended to think it over. "Oh, sometime around our fiftieth anniversary, you might ask me for another kiss."

He stood up, his expression as bland as if he hadn't said such an outlandish, bizarre, ridiculous thing. Way more annoying than her playful reminders about going into the street with Ian. Had he read her earlier expression, when she had been keeping any thought of his mouth on hers so carefully hidden? Sometimes he almost seemed to be so mentally close as to be able to read her emotions.

"Are you finished? Should we go in and free our parents from unpaid duty in our shops?"

Was she disappointed that the mouth moved away? Or irritated about the abrupt end of the conversation? She decided it was irritation at his silly insinuation that she might even be interested in anything like getting closer to that mouth. As for the rest of what he said, she could pretend she didn't hear it. She hurried to move away before he did.

He took her cup and carried it with his to a trash receptacle. "Tell your mom I'm sending Dad for two cups of chai. She should come out to enjoy the river."

Twisting her own mouth into an exaggerated grin, she waved good-bye and went into the shop. She really didn't care where the party was to be, and she found herself looking forward to it wherever it was. But if Mitch Williams thought she would beg him for anything, including a kiss by that mouth, he was crazy. He'd been acting as if he could read her mind since that first day that Little Bit came in, and it was time he learned that he was wrong.

She wasn't surprised that Julia refused to leave the shop to drink tea with Owen Williams. In fact, she wasn't surprised that Owen Williams didn't appear with cups of tea, but only walked by with a friendly wave. Perhaps he already knew her mother pretty well.

It was just after dusk when the members of the band called for her and Julia at the shop door, telling her only to bring her fiddle. Cassie first noted that Danny was with them but The Siren From the Sea wasn't, and then reprimanded herself for letting this woman's presence or absence make a difference. She looked at the laughing faces surrounding her and determined that she was going to enjoy this night even if The Siren should appear later.

Rosie was waiting to walk with them

when they came out and, as Cassie was escorted down the River Walk, Owen and Mitch joined them, both dressed in casual tees and jeans, as were the rest of the men. Mitch had a tan angora sweater draped across his shoulders.

They played as they walked. Cassie raised her fiddle and let it slip in whenever she thought it would add to the sound.

She forgot about The Siren, about money worries and the shop being closed early, and any possible evil Williams's plot. She just enjoyed the sensations: of lights and greenery, scents from open-air restaurants, and the happy applause from people sitting there as they walked by playing their instruments.

She wasn't even concerned with the eventual site for the party, but she was delighted when they turned into La Villita. She hadn't taken time to visit this combination of craft and serious art quarter since she had come to San Antonio.

They finished their music with a flourish and then parted to go into whichever of the arts and crafts places each chose in the tiny town within a town. Cassie announced briefly that no one was to buy her a present, and, considering the known financial situation of most of them, she knew they wouldn't argue.

She found herself between Mitch and Ian Weaver as she turned into a small gallery filled with paintings of various views of the River Walk, ranging from the stark patterns of individual trees during the short period of loss of leaves, to boats full of happy people, to poignant studies of individuals. One painting of a rainbow over the river reminded her of the happy murals in the church basement.

"Oh, look at this one," Cassie stopped before a miniature of an extremely old man sitting alone on one of the steps by the river, a mélange of colors that indicated the splendor of the River Walk's natural beauty behind him. "How can he look so sad with that background of beauty? It's heartbreaking."

"I think," Ian answered, seriously, "that he is sad because he is no longer capable of appreciating or walking about in that beauty."

For a moment, Cassie was surprised that Ian responded as he did, then she understood. For Ian the whole meaning of life was appreciating all kinds of beauty, whether sounds or sights or relationships. The thief who took his wallet but played the harmonica superbly ran through her mind.

She didn't look at Mitch but allowed his lack of response to rest uneasily on her mind. Did he feel no reaction at all to the painting?

After a while, Owen Williams and Benny found them and gathered them together. When they came out of the gallery Cassie realized that her mother had been optimistic about the weather and her blouse and skirt. She gave a surprised little shiver. Immediately, she felt the soft warmth of Mitch's sweater settle over her shoulders.

"I figured you'd need it after seeing that outfit," he murmured close to her ear.

Cassie was torn between the lovely softness of the sweater, irritation at his assuming he knew what was best for her, and a grudging happiness that he chose to consider her comfort, knowing that she had deliberately provoked him with her reminder of the afternoon playing music in the street with Ian. Ian seemed not to be noticing the interaction between them. Almost as if he had drifted mentally away from them for a while.

Owen and Benny gathered them all together and shepherded them down to sit in a stepped amphitheater and watch a presentation of *A Christmas Carol* by a group of talented local actors on a stage that was across the river. Ian came out of whatever place he had drifted into and sat beside her, making enjoyable small asides during the play, but Mitch had disappeared and didn't come back until well into the presentation. Though the group had thoughtfully left room beside Cassie, he sat with Julia instead of working his way down beside her. Cassie was happy to be enjoying the show with Ian. Happier than if Mitch's presence beside her might have taken her attention off the show.

As she watched Scrooge learn his lessons in a series of imaginatively staged ghostly visits, Cassie realized that Owen was paying for all this. Most of the group was consistently broke, with the exception perhaps of Benny Karcher, who spent his days doctoring sick engines and paid a salary to Keith Thomas.

Owen and Rosie were sitting in front of her, talking constantly in low, mostly unintelligible voices throughout the play. But one blip of their conversation caused Cassie to catch her breath and hold it while she listened.

"Mitch had to talk me into even coming down the first time to see this town he loves so much, but I understand now why he feels this way. And I'm behind him one hundred percent. I want to get a real store started. Music, art, readings from famous authors. Like my stores back East."

The music rose on the stage across the river, and Cassie didn't hear Rosie's response, but the magic of the evening was over. So, it was true. The friendliness of the Williams men, father and son, really was all a play. All to get Rosie and her to give in to their plans. Well, this would be one offer she could refuse, and she wasn't just thinking about their effort to buy her out. Mitch better not try to get closer to her, not in any way.

She tried not to let the overheard conversation keep her from sounding as enthusiastic as she wanted, as she thanked the group for her wonderful celebration, after the play ended and they started home. They peeled off at various steps to street level on the walk back. Ian gave Cassie a brief birthday kiss before he left. Only the Williamses and Julia were with her when they arrived at Teddy Bear's Christmas Shop. Ignoring the fact that Mitch was still beside them while his father had gone into the bookstore, Cassie unlocked her door, and her mother went in.

"Stay with me for a minute," Mitch said in a low tone. "I have something." He drew her to the bench outside.

And I know what that something actually is. But he won't be crass enough to tell me tonight. Then, why am I being naïve enough to stay with him? I won't think about his mouth. How is that mouth going to look if sometime in the future he knows that Teddy Bear's Shop has failed and I have to accept his offer?

"You're not really thinking about the way the river looks in the lights." His voice was thoughtful. She glanced at him. His mouth was close to hers.

"I'm not offering this as a penny for your thoughts," he added, taking a square object from his jacket pocket.

Cassie didn't have to look. It was the painting of the man who had spoken so compellingly to her from the miniature at La Villita.

He hardly let her speak a few words of thanks before he spoke again.

"He is an old spirit of La Villita, mourning for the Coahuiltecan Indians who can no longer live there, not for himself. That world by the river was their home for hundreds of years, and their spirit is still there. You felt it distilled in this one old man. I meant to get you something cheery, but this one is yours. It was meant for you."

Cassie looked down at the miniature to hide the tears that had sprung to her eyes. When she looked up, her own world was filled with the sight and feel of his mouth moving down toward her's.

It started as a gentle kiss. There was

no passion in it at first, almost only a rite of recognition of their mutual feeling for the history of this place, and of each other, but it was a long kiss. Slowly it changed, until his mouth on hers and his hands on her back pressing her closer to him blotted out the night, the river, and the buildings behind them—the buildings that contained their shops, the competing spaces. Cassie let herself forget them, thinking only of the ever-deepening pressure of his mouth against hers. She wasn't sure which of them ended the kiss. She knew that neither of them wanted to end it.

But he raised his head and looked down at her for a long moment, an unreadable expression on his face. "Cassie, believe that I only want what is best for you and me."

Too breathless to ask him to explain more, Cassie was ready to simply nod, not breaking the mood, when, glancing sideways, she saw the light flick off in

Rosie's coffee bar. Rosie. The sudden overwhelming memory of Owen Williams's words to Rosie earlier in the evening changed the whole meaning of his words—even of the kiss.

"I—I need to go in." His open look of disappointment told her that wasn't the response he wanted, but he only stood and walked with her to Teddy Bear's Shop door.

She was glad that her mother had gone on up to bed so she wouldn't have to try to make talk. Not while she was torn between the kiss and Rosie's allegations. It was while she was trying to sleep under a throw on her unopened couch that she allowed the wariness to take precedence. Mitch Williams might love the history and ambiance of this part of the world just enough to make him want to own as much of it as possible. And he was good at hiding his feelings. He had seemed not to respond at all when the three of them first saw the miniature and Ian saw only a tired old man. Instead he was accepting the agony of the spirit inside the man.

She finally went to sleep with Owen Williams's words in her mind instead of Mitch's. But the next morning, she remembered that, just as she was drifting off, she had decided where she was going to place the painting.

11

IAN CAME INTO the shop before noon. He took time for a few words with Julia about the evening before, but it was obvious that his whole mind wasn't on the conversation.

"Cassie, can you come for a walk?"

Cassie looked toward the door to see if he had left a musical instrument there. "For a little street music?" she asked. "Was our last stroll so successful?"

He grinned, a strained oddity of a grin. "Just a walk. Have you finished celebrating your birthday yet?"

Cassie looked at Julia. Her expression told her that she had picked up on Ian's uneasiness as well. She shooed the two of them out of the shop.

"Have lunch while you're out," she said. "I think Cassie is turning pale from staying in and eating cheese sandwiches. Don't worry about the shop, Cassie. I promise not to move anything—well, not many things. I might put a few things out in plainer sight."

"Okay, Mom. Be good to the cat." Cassie slipped into the workroom for her wallet.

"I feel like a kid being sent out to play," she said, as they strolled past Rosie's shop, noticing that Rosie had stopped making a drink for a large woman to watch them go by. She made another attempt to lighten the atmosphere. "But I do want to tell you how much I enjoyed the surprise party last night."

"Everyone did," he answered, with an obvious effort to sound warmer than his unusual demeanor was showing. "It's not really fair to call it your party when we had as much fun as you did," he added.

Cassie was unsure how to answer.

His expression, the feeling she was getting of tightly coiled muscles, all belied his words. She took the opportunity of slapping him lightly on the arm, finding it to be as tense as she suspected. "No, I demand that it be my party. If it had bombed you could have called it everyone's."

She immediately regretted the words. It was becoming too apparent that for him, something in the evening had gone wrong.

He rubbed his arm in pretended pain, carefully going along with her. "Okay, it's only yours." His smile was only a tight movement of his mouth, going nowhere near his eyes.

They walked in silence for a short period, Cassie wanting urgently to help her friend cope with whatever was disturbing him but feeling unable to hone in on his extraordinary mood. Ian had seemed to be a laid-back, let's-enjoy-life kind of person. Cassie didn't know how to accept this unknown someone who was walking beside her.

He seemed to suddenly realize the tension between them and made an effort to ease it. "Let's go up to the street and find a hot dog stand. I have a definite length of time that I can miss eating a hotdog. The clock just rolled over to my control limit."

Cassie agreed, respecting his lack of pretense about what he could afford and feeling the same way about her own finances. Once up on the street, they walked several blocks before they found a stand. Ian watched as she chose everything on her hotdog, and then he did the same; he made no argument when she paid for her own. They concentrated on juggling their plastic containers, sacks of chips, and soft drinks as they searched for an empty bench somewhere, finally carrying everything back to the little park outside the Alamo. Since it was early for lunch, not many of the brown-baggers were out, and tourists were still walking about the grounds, so there were several empty benches there.

She was hungry and, after the usual struggle to open the plastic bag, took a big bite of potato chip to start the meal with something salty. She was holding a chip on her tongue for the lasting enjoyment when she became aware that he had put his food down on the bench beside him without tasting it.

Searching out his mood, she felt his discomfort and hesitancy seem to increase. It was so unlike the open Ian she had seen before to be unsure of himself, or of what he wanted to say.

She waited a while for him to tell her what was on his mind, and then decided to help. Something in the atmosphere between them had to change, and since he had asked her to come with him, he must want to tell her what had happened. She wanted him to know that she was willing to share whatever was disturbing him.

"You didn't ask me out here just to eat hotdogs, did you?"

He shook his head, and this time she waited in silence for him to find the words he wanted to use. "I went down to La Villita this morning to see if Nerina would give me a really good discount on the painting you liked so well last night. She said it was sold. Mitch bought it for you, didn't he?"

Cassie choked, struggling not to spray bits of chip around. When she could get her breath, she sputtered, "Nerina? She runs that gallery?"

He turned away from her, concentrating on picking his hotdog up without spilling its fillings. Then, just holding it loosely in his hand without taking a bite, he turned back to watch her intently.

"You don't know."

Cassie took a swallow of her drink. It felt as if the whole chip was still in her throat. "I'm sorry. I'm not following you. Know what? What should I know? I suppose I must have accepted that she had to do something for a living. I just didn't connect her with that gallery."

Her concern for Ian changed to a strange dread that told her she didn't want to hear what he was about to say. Was he going to tell her of something to do with Mitch's involvement with Nerina? For a moment she let a memory of Mitch's kiss last night fill her mind. Did he kiss her while thinking of what was surely the sexiest mouth in the world? Did that kiss come anywhere near meaning to him what it did to her?

Ian set his hotdog back on the bench again. His discomfort with whatever he had to tell her was painful to watch. "That gallery where we saw the painting is hers. She doesn't run the gallery, Cassie. She's the artist. That painting. Of the old man. It's Nerina's work."

"Nerina?" Cassie felt as if she were an echo.

"She's an outstanding artist. Way

above outstanding. But she doesn't believe in herself. She can't accept herself as she is, so she keeps trying to change herself into something she can like."

Cassie couldn't concentrate on anything he said about Nerina's emotional problems. Not yet. "And you went there with me and didn't tell me? You and Mitch both. How could you? Either of you?"

He didn't answer her directly. "She talked about the painting to me this morning. She's feeling nostalgic about letting it go. It's not really about a man. It's mourning the Indians who lived there at La Villita and are gone. She claims Indian blood. She didn't know who bought it."

Cassie clutched her hotdog too tightly in her hand, looking at it as if it were something distasteful. A bite would choke her. It wasn't that Mitch understood the spiritual heart of the painting last night because he was sensitive to her emotions.

He knew. Nerina had told him what she meant by it. And he had the nerve to give it to her without telling her who painted it. Both of the men with her knew it was Nerina's work and didn't tell her.

She felt sick as she asked, "But she knows now?"

Ian nodded. "Who probably bought it. I'm glad Mitch gave it to you, if he did. I watched your face while you studied it. It was meant for you to have it."

"He did." Cassie watched the relish dripping out of the crumbling bun onto the bench between them, without doing anything to catch it. She wanted to finish this lunch. She needed to get away from this conversation and back to impersonal work in the shop. She was meant to have an expensive painting done by Nerina Smith? The Siren From the Sea? A painting Mitch had bought for her without telling her the truth about it? She might decide that the best place for it was face down on a table. Or put away in a drawer. But Ian was right about the painting. It was more than good. It not only showed the beauty of the river, it created a mood that spilled through any memory of it. Even now, appalled by Mitch's deceitful action in giving it to her, the mood of the painting remained.

Then she remembered something Ian had said to her when she first saw Nerina. "Is that what you meant by 'there's more' when we were talking about Nerina that first night I played with the band?"

He looked puzzled, then shrugged. "Probably. Yes. There's more to Nerina than that ridiculous persona she's wearing now. She's worn other personas at other times. She even lived as a street person. She's still in contact with many of them. She probably could tell me where my wallet is this minute if she wanted to."

"Who is she, then, and why mask herself in different personas? And why go to the trouble of keeping her painting a secret from me?"

"She knew Mitch was bringing you to play with us, and she was angry about it. Jealous of you before she even met you. That's one reason why she made us promise not to tell you anything about her. The other one is bigger. She used to live in Dallas. She was in jail there for stealing some stuff with her husband of that time. She had a baby in jail, and her husband took it. She never saw the baby or the husband again. It made the news, and she was afraid you might recognize her. She made us agree not to tell you anything about her. Just Sarah and Mitch and I know who she really is. Sarah's minister tried to work with her. You know him, don't you?"

Cassie nodded. "I heard him one Sunday."

"Nerina walked away from their meetings. She couldn't accept anyone getting inside her mask."

A memory of a rainbow slipped through Cassie's mind. Two rainbows.

One at the gallery and one on the walls of the church basement.

"She did the mural in the church basement? For the children?"

"Yes. While she was in counseling with the minister."

"And Mitch paid for it?"

"She did it free. She's crazy about kids. She still hurts from losing her own child. A lot of her wildness now is to cover up for that hurt. It's hard to explain Nerina. She tries to wrap herself in the nonconforming artist person. But she's so unsure of her own talent that she just can't allow herself to be called an artist to anyone she calls strangers."

"You're sure you're talking about the same Nerina Smith I've seen?"

He was silent for a moment. "No, I'm not talking about that same person. There is no same person. I met Nerina when I wandered into her gallery one afternoon. And she was wearing jeans and a big shirt. Being the casual artist who didn't care about clothes at that time. She changed into another of her personalities after I brought her to be with me while the band played. After I introduced her to Mitch. She thinks she needs that Siren From the Sea persona you saw. She thinks that's the only way she can attract him."

Neither of them even pretended to be eating. "And she needs Mitch?"

"She thinks she does. She doesn't really know Mitch. She just sees this handsome man who writes. Who has money. She doesn't know what she needs yet. Some day she will. And when she does, I'll be there."

Cassie felt her mouth drop open and took a tiny bite of her smashed hotdog to give it something to do. Ian was speaking of his own feelings for Nerina. The Nerina he was telling her she didn't know and therefore mustn't judge.

She was barely able to chew the bite and swallow. She dropped the rest of the hotdog into the sack, pushing a napkin half-heartedly at the slippery leavings between her fingers.

Ian picked up her sack, dropped the hotdog he hadn't tasted in with it, and left her abruptly to find a trashcan. When he came back, he changed the subject, making Cassie feel as if she were suddenly coming back to an ordinary world where people walked around them doing tourist things, and where she was not yet ready to be.

"Only one more practice before the big trip down the river. You'll come to Benny's tomorrow night? Bring your mom."

Cassie frowned as she stood, and then tried to answer in as offhand tone as the one he had suddenly adopted.

"I'll come. I don't know about Mom. Ian, you don't need to walk back with me. Not that I don't enjoy your company," she added hastily.

He smiled, a ghost of a smile. "Okay.

I'll see Mitch tomorrow night, but I'm not quite yearning to run into him right now."

"Neither am I," Cassie agreed. She watched Ian's back as he walked away. Nerina Smith wasn't the only one who was different from the person she thought she had met in the band. She let herself wonder for a moment what the inner stories of the other members might be. Then she went back to her shop without seeing anything around her, or thinking about where she was going.

Back in the Teddy Bear's Shop, she threw herself into a constant movement of rearranging and neatening the merchandise when she wasn't busy helping a customer. She didn't want any time to think about the things she'd learned from Ian. Or to remember Mitch's kiss. Occasionally she caught her mother looking at her with a question in her expression, but Julia had never forced her to talk until she was ready even when she had been a teenager and madly in love with the same football player all the cheerleaders drooled over.

Once she stopped and stood holding a handful of candles as her mother's look told her she was picking up merchandise Julia had just put on display. Her mother only nodded as she put them back in the original basket, making no comment.

Later Cassie brought the subject of the band practice up with Julia as they were closing the register after a good sales day. "We always practice after we close our businesses, so it gets a little late. But come with me tomorrow night. You'll enjoy it."

Julia picked a snowman up and stood looking down at it, and then turned toward Cassie, her expression showing a mental struggle to ask what had happened to her daughter, against her knowledge that Cassie was an adult who kept her own counsel. Finally, she just hugged

LOUISE COLLN

Cassie with the snowman still in her hand, holding her tightly for a few moments.

Cassie managed a smile. "Mom, you're sticking the snowman into my neck."

Julia stood back. "I believe this little fat guy liked being held by that angel. I'll put him back."

"And you'll come listen to us practice?"

"I believe I will. It should be fun."

THE BAND MEMBERS were a little more sober than usual, as they earnestly prepared for the trip down the river. Owen Williams was there with Mitch, and he and Julia sat together listening to the band. Perhaps, Cassie thought, they had made a sort of peace at the birthday party. She was glad that she had decided to wait to tell Julia what she had heard between Owen and Rosie. Or what she had learned about Nerina. They didn't need an overflowing volcano just now. She was having enough trouble keeping her questions about Mitch in some kind of limbo while they concentrated on playing.

Nerina wasn't there. Perhaps she was sulking after learning from Ian who had the painting. Cassie wondered if Nerina and Mitch had discussed it. She stopped herself, realizing that she'd missed hearing her cue to come in and they had gone on without her. She couldn't respond to Mitch's meant-to-be comforting wink or Ian's understanding half-smile as she worked her way back into the arrangement. After they agreed to meet the next evening at the boat landing, she hurried Julia out with only a wave to Sarah, ignoring Mitch and Ian. She wasn't ready to talk to either of them.

Riding home in her mother's car, Cassie didn't feel ready to respond to Julia's carefully conceived, non-intrusive interest in yesterday's walk with Ian and the mood that Cassie was unable to conceal when she returned to Teddy Bear's Shop. Cassie allowed some curiosity of her own to ask how Julia and Owen had enjoyed the practice.

"And if we talked to each other?" Julia asked, turning her gaze from the street for a moment to give Cassie an "I know what you're really asking" look.

"Well, that too," Cassie admitted.

Julia turned her attention back to the scant traffic at that time of night. "Yes, we did. He told me a bit about his divorce, without blaming his ex-wife, as most of the men my age that I've met do. He's very lonely. He pretty much lives for Mitch and his daughter back in the East. Them and his business."

She moved a hand from the wheel for an instant, then clenched it back and applied the brakes in an unusually jerky style at a red light. "That only makes me more absolutely sure we need to watch him. And listen to Rosie."

Cassie looked to see if someone was

crowding Julia's car or stopping suddenly in front of them, then realized it was her mother's reaction to the possibility of Owen's intentions about Teddy Bear's Shop that had caused the rough stop.

Then her own thoughts surprised her. Owen Williams lonely? He seemed to be one of the most social persons she had met recently. She drifted into such deep thought she wasn't even aware of their silence as her surprise to learn of unexpected emotions in Owen turned her back to Ian and Nerina—and Mitch.

They walked the short distance to her apartment from the parking garage in a pensive silence, and their good nights before Julia went into the bedroom were subdued.

In her living room Cassie stopped preparing her couch for bed to pick up the mourning man painting and study it for a long time, finding a few tiny Indian paint brush flowers suspended in the greenery behind him. Then, letting her hands make the decision, she opened that small drawer in her dining table and slid the miniature in, turned down on top of her bills.

Did Mitch know that Nerina knew whom he had bought it for?

12

FOR THE CHRISTMAS river trip Cassie chose a long swishy skirt, with tiny Santas and reindeer dancing against a green background, and a matching top of soft cotton, while her mother tucked a classic red blouse into winter white pants. Cassie was glad that she and Mitch had agreed earlier to close their shops at eight, so there was no necessity to discuss anything with him now.

As she and Julia left Teddy Bear's Shop, Rosie waved good-bye to her boyfriend in the coffee bar and came out to walk with them. Owen and Mitch joined them when they went by the bookstore. Cassie inserted herself between Rosie, who was stuffed into a bright-green outfit, and Owen. Cassie pretended not to see the mystified look that Mitch gave her as he walked with a somewhat-less-than-friendly Julie, just as she had found a need to dash upstairs to her apartment the two times he had come into the shop earlier, leaving her mother to explain somehow.

Owen and Rosie carried on a conversation across Cassie, which she was grateful for but didn't listen to, being aware only that it had nothing to do with any of their places of business.

The rest of the band met them at the boat landing. Nerina walked up with Ian, looking subdued. On some faces it would have been a pout, Cassie thought, not surprised that Nerina ignored her presence, nor sensing any need to force a greeting. She was glad to see that Nerina was wearing a silk pantsuit, skin-tight but better for the boat than her usual costumes. It was subdued beige that blended into the Christmas colors the other women were wearing and made her, Cassie admitted to herself, seem more intellectual and less physical. The information Ian had given her probably helped in her changed—at least somewhat changed—conception of the woman. Yet she felt she should cease calling her The Siren From the Sea, since learning of the serious painting the woman did and Ian's feelings toward her. But why call her anything? She stifled consideration of taking a trip alone to La Villita later, just to return the painting and get it out of her dining table drawer and out of her life.

Someone interrupted her thoughts to remind them that they should pose for their annual photo before boarding the boat. They grouped together amid good-natured arguments about who should stand in front. It took several minutes to get the band close enough to catch them in the picture with all their instruments, and longer to catch them all looking cheerful at the same time. Cassie couldn't help a feeling of relief that Nerina stood between Owen and Rosie, and that Mitch ended up beside Julia instead of her.

There was some nervous laughter as they boarded the boat, but they were generally feeling good, and Cassie determined to put everything out of her mind and enjoy the experience. They had put in hours working toward this night, as well as saving their money all year, only for the joy of playing Christmas music while floating on the river. They hoped to please whoever might be sitting or walking on the River Walk, but the greatest pleasure was to perform well in the ambiance of the river.

Since the whole boat rather than individual seats was rented, it was ready to take off as soon as they all trooped onto it and found their places. Owen had suggested bringing Little Bit along, but Mitch refused to consider pulling him out of the water again, and Cassie had nixed Julia's desire to bring the big teddy bear on the theory that it would be wrong to use the rest of the band to advertise her shop, no matter how much Julia had pointed out that she needed all the exposure she could get, and how much the children on the Walk would enjoy seeing the bear drift by.

Only Rosie, Owen, and Julia sat down. The others grouped themselves in the front of the shallow boat, more or less in the places they took when they practiced. Sarah and Mitch stood together, while Cassie stood beside Ian and Keith with their guitars. Benny took a place off to one side, from where he casually directed them. Nerina had moved to stand beside Mitch.

As soon as the man who drove from the back of the boat brought it well into the river, they swirled into a rousing interpretation of *God Rest Ye Merry, Gentlemen*. As people walking beside the river or sitting late at outdoor tables stopped to listen, they played a wild arrangement by Benny combining the two versions of *Joy to the World*, both the classic and the happy bullfrog, Jeremiah. The exhilarating music excited some of the walkers into a faster gait. Some walked along with the boat for a while, then dropped off as others followed them. Several couples walking together went into an impromptu dance.

Cassie hoped that Nerina would refrain from slipping into one of her own dance interpretations. She noticed Sarah and Benny looking at Nerina as if they might be worried, too. If she was aware of their concern, she didn't show it. Only a subdued movement of her hips kept her gently touching Mitch.

Waving often to the enthusiastic listeners on the River Walk, they repeated their mixture of instrumental arrangements and vocals, classic and modern carols, stopping before each bridge while Sarah and Mitch sang.

As Cassie played softly behind Sarah's

I'll Be Home for Christmas, she heard a harmonica blending with her harmony and felt Ian's hand on her shoulder.

"Don't stop playing, but look up. It's our highwayman."

Leaning on the bridge railing above them, the man, looking as unkempt as he had before, played with them. When Sarah had finished the song, Benny motioned for the man to play alone. He played a heartbreakingly melancholy version of *I'll Be Home for Christmas* and then faded into the crowd as the group on the boat led the applause of the people on the bridge.

"Afraid someone may have called the police while he played," Ian said. "But he'll come to the garage. He can't stay away."

"Right now," Cassie choked out, "I hope he finds his way back to home, wherever it is."

Something pulled her gaze to look directly into Mitch's eyes. Something deep in his expression almost made all her hurt feelings about the painting slip somewhere below her recognition. Here on this boat, even with Nerina beside him, she could believe that he really meant only the best for her.

Not taking time out to wipe tears from her eyes, she took up her fiddle to accompany the band, which was starting on a repeat of their repertoire as they played to other walkers while they floated under the myriad lights above them in the trees.

After they left the boat, they all piled into cars and trooped over to Sarah's house. Everyone was feeling happy and good about the evening. Only Nerina declined Sarah's invitation. Cassie considered that perhaps she felt that she couldn't blend with Sarah's unaffected hospitality. Or perhaps she was sulking about the painting.

Sarah's house, set behind an elaborate three-story brick, must have been servants' quarters at one time, Cassie decided. The doll-sized house was much too small for all of them, but they made room and enjoyed sandwiches and cake and each other's company. Cassie was too caught up in the spirit of the evening to let her uncertainty about Mitch's intentions—either on her shop or her mouth—keep her from enjoying the company, just glad that Nerina had chosen not to come.

While everyone was enjoying second pieces of cake, Cassie whispered to Sarah to come with her into the minuscule hall where a small tree was set up.

"I have something I want you to do for me," she said.

In the hall, she pulled the other angel from her pocket. "For Danny," she said. "My Christmas present."

"Oh, Cassie. You mustn't. You only had two."

"Please, I want Danny to find it hanging on his tree."

Sarah was a gracious person, and it

was obvious that the thought of Danny's enjoyment of the present was impossible to ignore. She hugged Cassie and accepted the angel.

Cassie didn't notice that Sarah was looking over her shoulder until she was suddenly aware that the other woman had slipped away. She turned to see why and found herself tucked against Mitch's shoulder.

"I've been trying to get you alone for two days now," he said, his breath stirring her hair as he held her too close to let her think of anything but the pleasure of his arms about her. "Are you really that busy?"

Reluctantly, she pushed herself back just enough to look eye to eye with him. "I've been hiding from you," she answered honestly.

"I judged as much. Why? That kiss made me feel closer to you. It seems to have made you feel way out in space somewhere. Any space away from me."

She pulled herself all the way from him. "Mitch, how can you ask why? It's because you weren't honest with me about the painting. And you aren't being honest with me now about your 'Why?' You have to know that I didn't know who did that painting and that I do know now."

He looked at her in puzzlement. "Does the painter make the painting less special? I gave it to you because you showed a connection with the man in the painting. You understood his emotion."

"You didn't tell me *she* painted it."

Finally, a light seemed to burst in his head. "You're jealous." He whooped in satisfaction. "You're jealous. I've never been sure how you're reacting to me, you're such an independent person, though you certainly returned my kiss, but now I know. You're jealous of Nerina."

"I am not. How can you think I'm jealous of her?" She took a step backward, and he followed her.

She barely had time to think that he wasn't answering her question as usual when she felt his hands cupping each side of her head while his mouth pressed hers into a meeting that drove all memory of Nerina away to make room in their world for just the two of them, Cassie and Mitch—no one else existed.

A gaggle of delighted laughs and calls interrupted them as the rest of the band crowded into the tiny hall, separating them and insisting on giving their own Merry Christmas kisses to Cassie and hugs among themselves. As she met Mitch's good-humored but frustrated gaze over Benny's shoulder, Cassie let her own expression tell him that she shared his feelings. They let the group shuffle them back into the living room, where the party broke up.

Rosie asked for a ride in Mitch's sports car for her Christmas present, and Mitch couldn't refuse her. Owen drove home with Cassie and Julia. Cassie sat in the back seat, hearing the buzz of conversation between Julia and Owen but not really listening except to hear Owen say he was catching a late-night plane to spend Christmas with his daughter in Connecticut.

"Red-eye special," he said. "All the others are full the day before Christmas. My daughter, both my children, are very important to me," he said. "Mitch and I will have our Christmas together tonight." He laughed. "No more food, though. And not late, considering that plane he's helping me catch." Julia's answer was a murmur.

At home, Cassie and Julia readied for bed without talking much, only saying that they needed to get up early for the last day of Christmas shopping. The happy haze that had encircled Cassie since Mitch's kiss kept her from going to sleep for a long time after she heard Julia's gentle snores coming from the bedroom. It wasn't until she was drifting off that she suddenly remembered that Mitch hadn't ever really explained Nerina, and she wondered, if Owen was leaving, was Mitch spending Christmas with that woman?

She must have been asleep for a while, but she wasn't sure why she thought that, wandering in a haze of not knowing if she was awake or dreaming. A dream in which she seemed to hear small noises in the room with her.

Half awake, she heard herself calling out softly, "Mitch? Mitch?"

She came fully awake to the feel of a hand on her shoulder and a low voice close to her ear.

"Don't scream. Don't talk. I ain't Mitch."

She opened her eyes. The room was in darkness, but she could feel the shape of a face just above hers and a solid bulk beside her. Frightened as she was, her mind registered that the near-whisper was friendly and relaxed. Was one of the band playing a trick on her? Maybe pretending to be Santa Claus? Then, a nose-clogging odor told her it wasn't one of them.

"Who is it? What are you doing here?"

A long, drawn-out sigh blew alcohol into her face. "You never do as you're told. Well, at least you didn't scream. Maybe you're learning how to act when someone has a knife."

She sat up and felt him jerk back. "You. Harmonica player. How did you get in here?"

"Lady, these old locks know when a master's hand is working on them. It wasn't any trouble at all. You make any more sudden moves, and you're gonna stab yourself on this knife. I'm trying not to hurt you."

"What do you want?"

"Keep it low, lady. I figure if you're sleeping on the couch, Mama's sleeping in the bedroom, and we don't want her to hear us, do we? Don't worry. I don't have any intentions on your person. I just want to pick up a painting, and then we'll go downstairs for a while."

"Painting? Why does someone—"

"Someone like me want a painting like that? Well, lady, maybe I want to hang it on the wall under my bridge. Just tell me where it is. You don't have it out. I've already looked every place I can find."

"It's in a drawer over there." She flipped her hand toward the dining table on the other side of the room. "In the dining table. It's not easy to see." Now that her eyes were getting adjusted she could make out the form of her familiar furniture beyond his body.

"You've got to stop making sudden movements. Don't you have a *How to Be a Burglary Victim for Idiots* book? Maybe I should write one. Now get up slowly and walk to the table with me. Being very careful to not crash against anything loud enough to stop that snoring from the next room."

It wasn't worth risking a knife wound to keep the painting; even if she was sure she still wanted it now that she knew its origin. She moved carefully as she was told, missing the foot of the table, which had earlier caught her toe painfully. She opened the drawer and put the painting in his hand.

"Now will you leave?"

He slipped the painting into an outside pocket of his jacket. "Now you will just as carefully get your keys and walk down the stairs with me, missing any creaks on the way."

"Why? I'm in my pajamas."

"I don't care, and you'll see why." A hand on her arm stopped her as he listened for the continuing snoring from the bedroom.

She didn't need light to pick up the keys. She kept them where they'd be right by her hand when she got up each morning. But he brought out a tiny-beamed flashlight after they were on the stairway. The stairs were quiet under their feet. Hers were bare, and he seemed to be wearing something soft. He put each foot down carefully, touching only his toes to the bare wood of the stairs. The door to the shop made only a tiny creak. Was it enough to wake Julia?

"Close the door. Lock it."

Cassie did as she was told. "You're going to rob me?"

He shook his head. "My benefactor doesn't want any of these trinkets to get onto the market so they can be traced. Things are just going to get broken. Sit over there by your cash register. Guard it from me." His laugh was almost friendly.

"You're going to trash my shop? How can you? I cried for you when you played with us from the bridge."

"Thank you, ma'am. I appreciate that. Then you'll be glad to know that with what I make for this job, I can kiss this town good-bye for good tomorrow. Maybe even find me a home somewhere. With a woman pretty as you." He looked at her for a moment. "Lady, I like you. I would have just let you sleep while I did this except for needing to find that picture."

"Who's paying you to do this? You've got to tell me who's paying you. Is it the people next door? Is it?" She thought she couldn't bear to hear the answer.

"Might be some connection there." He didn't answer otherwise. He took a small hammer and a bottle of some kind of liquid out of his pockets and set to work smashing ceramics. It was while he poured whatever liquid he had onto a basket of plush bears and reindeer that Cassie had enough. She tiptoed toward his back, unsure of what she would do but determined not to let him do more damage to her shop.

Even with his back turned, he seemed to know she was behind him. Twisting quickly and dropping the bottle of liquid to splash across the carpet, he flung her to the floor. In the next moment, he reached down to help her up, in spite of her angry attempts to roll away from him.

"Lady, I keep telling you, I don't want to hurt you. Just get up and go back to that register. You know I can't put this knife down, and I may lose control if you keep acting like this."

As she stood, tears of disappointed anger in her eyes, the lights of a police car flashed on the street above. He looked up and then turned back to her.

"Uh-oh. Mama must have woke up. Just open the door for me." He slipped his hammer into his pocket and caught up the bottle of unknown fluid and held it against her cheek. "The outside one. To the River Walk."

Feeling something stinging on her cheek from the dripping bottle, she did as she was told and watched in angry frustration as he blended into the night shadows of the River Walk. She caught one last glimpse of him running. Then she unlocked the stairway door and the police and Julia came in, Julia hugging her and pleading with her to say she was unharmed.

"I woke when you opened the door to the shop," she said. "I thought you couldn't sleep and may have come down to work in the shop, and I came down to help you. But then I heard you talking and heard him smashing things, and the door was locked. I guess he was making so much noise he didn't hear me try to open it, so I went back and called the police."

Cassie returned her mother's hugs, assuring her that she was unhurt while not interrupting Julia's nervous flow of words. The police interview and evaluation of the damage took the little bit left of the night.

The police were brutally honest about chances of finding the man. "If the painting comes on the market, maybe we can trace the seller. We can take fingerprints."

Cassie thought a while. "I don't believe he actually touched anything except the painting. And he took that with him."

They had barely left when Mitch came in. "Cassie, what happened? I just got back from taking Dad to the airport." He looked at the ceramic pieces scattered around, then at Cassie, still in her baggy pajamas, standing in the middle of the jumble, unable to concentrate on doing anything about it. For a minute a twitch of a tender smile played about his face. It changed immediately to acute concern as he came toward her.

"Are you all right?"

His question included her mother.

Cassie stepped back away from him. "How convenient that you had a reason not to be here. How thoughtful that you waited for the police to leave. You tell me what happened." She could feel the words tearing from her throat. "You sent him. He said so. He said that you were involved."

He followed her, attempting to put his arms around her. "What? Cassie, make sense."

She shook him off angrily. "I knew that you knew what the painting was about when Ian told me Nerina painted it. She told you what the man was mourning. If you decided you didn't want me to have it, why didn't you ask me for it? I would have given it back if you'd asked. I'd have been glad to. Glad to get rid of it. You didn't have to send him to steal it."

He looked sincerely puzzled. *He's not just a golden boy. He's a great actor.* Cassie tried not to hear his proclamation of innocence. "Is the painting gone? And what does it have to do with any of this?" He waved his arm toward the crushed ceramics. "Whatever makes you think I sent someone to steal the painting?"

"He said so. I asked him who paid him to steal the painting and trash my shop and he said you did."

Mitch tried one more time to hold Cassie, while Julia just looked on, seeming as if she was wishing she could be anywhere but here, but not in any way attempting to help Mitch.

"I can't believe this. You're exhausted, Cassie. You were scared last night. You didn't hear what you thought you heard. Let me help you clean this up, and we can get the shop opened even today. You can't afford to miss the last day before Christmas." He looked around. "We just have to take out this basket of animals." He lifted the basket and sniffed it. "It smells like alcohol. Did he pour it on anything else? I'll get a broom and dustpan from the bookstore."

"You just go back to your store and stay there. I believed you weren't trying to drive me out when Little Bit first came and when he messed things up in here, and I almost believed you didn't stop up my sink, or make Rosie's coffee spill"— ignoring the fact that he wasn't there when Rosie spilled the coffee on her rug—"or kept the shelves and the dolls from coming, but I heard what I heard last night. You noticed that this is the last day before Christmas. What a good day to trash my shop. Well, you just better learn that I'm tougher than you think. You can't drive me out. I will open today, and I'll stay open, too, in spite of you."

He seemed to finally understand that she was serious. He stepped back, his face suddenly stiff. "Cassie, if you can really believe I would do this—" He indicated the mess with another sweep of his hand, stopped talking for a moment, and then seemed to start again. "If you can really believe I would do such a thing to anyone, especially you—" He hesitated again. "You're right. I should go."

He turned and walked toward the door.

"And keep that cat away, too," Cassie called after his back.

He barely turned his head. "I knew what the painting meant by my research into Texas history and the stories of the Indians that I'm writing."

He didn't look back at her again.

Julia had been standing by the cash register, watching. Now she strode forward. "He's right about one thing, Cassie. There's not much real damage. We'll get the shop open today. And this has opened your eyes. Maybe Mitch didn't know about this. He looked really confused. Maybe Owen Williams did. Maybe that's why he went back to Connecticut for Christmas. If he'd already set it up, then—I was beginning to think I was wrong about them, too." She went silent, seeing Cassie's face. "I think Rosie's open now. I'll bring some coffee. We're going to need it today." She carried the basket of animals out to the trash as she went.

When she was gone, Cassie got down on her knees with a small wastebasket, picking up pieces of her decorations. It was several minutes before she became aware that tears were running down the dried alcohol on her cheek, making it sting slightly again. She stopped working and bent her head to the floor, sobbing. She was still there when Julia came back in with coffee. Julia put the coffee by the register and knelt beside her.

"Cassie, you're exhausted. Go up and sleep a while. I'll finish cleaning up and open the shop."

Cassie shook her head, rising to her knees, and taking a stinging gulp of the hot coffee. "I couldn't sleep, Mom. Let's just get this place open." She looked at the new stain stretching across the carpet and almost laughed. "Do you know anyone who sells carpet stain removal by the barrel? I seem to need it."

Julia answered practically about removing the stain, giving Cassie space to bring herself to some kind of control, since she wouldn't go upstairs.

Finally, Cassie did go up, just long enough to get into her day clothes. They opened almost on time, before the surge of shoppers and lookers hit the Walk and the malls. Cassie tried not to look at the empty bear's lap as people wandered in and out.

A woman with a little girl came in about mid-morning.

"Where's the cat, Mommy?" the little girl whined. "You said we'd see a cat if we came out. I want to go back and watch TV."

The mother scowled at Cassie. "So where is the cat? You can't let people think they'll see the cat and then not have him here."

Cassie managed to suppress a reply that the cat and everything else from next door would never set foot in Teddy Bear's Shop again by mentally reviewing her mantra of Public, Public, Public.

"Try in the bookstore next door," she said gently. "Little Bit divides his time between us."

"Well, it certainly seems that you'd have more concern for your customers." The woman flounced out, dragging the whining little girl by the hand. Cassie watched her go, thinking that sending them over to Mitch had made her feel a little better. Then she turned away from an incoming woman to wipe the returning tears from her eyes.

13

CASSIE WAS AWAKE much of the night, glad that after a while she heard soft snoring coming from the bedroom where her mother slept. In the morning, a glance at the covers on the made-up sofa told both of them of Cassie's restlessness, though neither of them commented on it.

They each had secretly chosen Christmas gifts for the other on their trip to El Mercado. The short time spent unwrapping and enjoying Julia's collector plate and the mate to Cassie's dragon was a much-needed respite from their despondency.

"I'm putting the dragons on my table in the dining area," Cassie said, hugging her mother. "And I may share my cheese sandwiches with them."

"The plate will go on my dining room wall, so we can each think of the other while we eat," Julia answered. "Now go back to sleep and don't get up till you smell the turkey. You know how much I enjoy making holiday meals."

"Sure. I also know that's the only cooking you enjoy," Cassie said, aware of how thin the veneer of Christmas cheer was for both of them.

She felt drugged from the unusual daytime sleep when her mother called her. Julia had created a small feast from a frozen turkey breast and a Southern sweet potato casserole with other fixings. But they ate mostly in a thoughtful silence, giving up on the pretense they had been trying for earlier.

After the meal, Cassie hugged her mother. "Mom, I couldn't have made it if you weren't here. Thank you so much for coming. I hate to see you leave tomorrow."

Julia hugged her back. "Then you'll be pleased to know that I'm not leaving. I called Helen while you were sleeping. She can handle the shop in Dallas a few more days. We need to do your markdowns early tomorrow. Now, do you want to see a movie or sleep some more while I put all these leftovers away?"

Cassie looked at the barely touched meal. "I'm sorry there's so many leftovers. It was a delicious meal."

Julia shrugged. "We'll have a lot of turkey sandwiches. I had thought I might invite—" She hesitated, as if aware that she had forgotten what a mention of Mitch might do. "some of the band today but—" She let the sentence hang.

"It's okay." Cassie didn't define what she meant, and her mother only nodded as she went on. "Can you understand? I want to go to sleep again. I know it's a get-away thing now, but—"

"Of course I understand. But you have to accept what has happened, eventually."

"I know."

"And you will," Julia went on, as though Cassie hadn't spoken. "You're my daughter, and you're strong."

Cassie managed a grin. "Like mother, like daughter. I'm going to stretch out on your bed so you can watch TV if you want."

Julia nodded, carrying their plates to the dishwasher. "I've got a pecan pie for later. With ice cream. And I'm taking a plate to Rosie. She's open today. So don't jump up screaming if you hear me coming and going."

Cassie managed a sliver of a smile. "You'd feed the world if you could."

Julia's answering smile turned into a wry frown. "Call me narrow-minded, but right now, I'd leave out your neighbors on the other side."

Cassie refused to recognize the gash of pain somewhere inside her body at the thought of Mitch. "I'm sorry not to be having a better time for Christmas."

Julia squeezed her shoulder. "Okay, sweetie, let him go for now. Just have good dreams."

But Cassie couldn't succeed in putting Mitch out of her mind. Every time she closed her eyes the intruder walked into her room again. Once she drifted into a half-sleep and the man played a tune on his harmonica, inviting her to put words to it—words saying over and over that Mitch was involved in the trashing of her shop. When she emerged from the half-dream, she went in to sit with her mother in front of the TV. In spite of her struggles not to, she saw it through the vision of Mitch's face or the man with the harmonica.

She didn't sleep much better that night and went the next morning with her mother down to the shop feeling as if someone had tied a scarf too tightly around her head.

Sarah called shortly after they came down. Julia called Cassie to the phone and went about the details of opening the shop while they talked.

"Cassie, I'm so sorry that man trashed your shop. How much damage did he do?"

Cassie couldn't keep the suspicion out of her voice. "How did you know about it?"

"Your mother called me yesterday. She thought you might have been asleep, and I told her not to wake you, and I'd call you today." The sound of Sarah's softly comforting voice made Cassie feel ashamed. What had happened to her that she was suspecting people like Sarah of conspiring against her? Then she realized that Sarah was still talking.

"I've known Mitch Williams for several years. I don't know why this thing happened, but I think the man in your shop was lying. Mitch was very kind to me when my baby died and when my husband left. Kinder than he needed to be for just another member of the band.

I can't accuse him of trying to ruin your business."

"I can." Cassie didn't even try to keep the bitterness out of her voice.

Sarah seemed to understand that Cassie wasn't ready to accept any defense of Mitch. "I have something else I want to tell you," she said. "Danny and I just hugged each other and cried a little together when he opened your angel gift. It took me some time to make him realize that the other angel was still on his sister's grave. Cassie, your gesture in giving him that angel was so sweet. I will never forget it or the close moments Danny and I had together. Moments that you gave us. I'm so sorry that your own Christmas was disappointing after what you gave to us."

Cassie assured her that she delighted in Danny's reception of the angel and listened as Sarah added her comforting words.

"I truly believe that somehow the pain you're feeling now will be better."

Cassie thanked her and hung up feeling that Sarah's friendship was a gift she could keep no matter what else happened.

She reported the conversation to Julia, who merely said that she had thought it would be better to wait to mention that she had talked with Sarah until Cassie could talk with her. Cassie repeated Sarah's insistence that Mitch wouldn't do such a thing.

"That's sure different from what Rosie thinks," Julia responded. "She gave me an earful this morning when I went over for more coffee. Owen Williams has been upping the ante for her space."

Cassie didn't expect Mitch to come anywhere near, but she was disappointed that none of the other members of the band contacted her. Surely Sarah had told them what had happened to the shop. Had they all chosen up sides already, and was the chosen one Mitch? After all, he had been with them longer. Cassie had thought that Ian, at least, had become friends with her, friends enough to want her to feel supported.

Even Little Bit stayed away. Kept away forcibly, Cassie assumed, not allowing herself to admit that she had grown fond enough of the brute to miss him. The shop was full of customers enjoying Julia's markdowns all day, and Cassie tried to get pleasure from the best business day since her opening. Many of her customers asked about the cat and were politely sent next door.

During a slowdown in traffic, she went to Rosie's for an afternoon break of latte and the chocolate cookies she found herself craving. She was struggling with the plastic wrapper on her cookie when she realized that Rosie looked like a boiling-over teapot.

Rosie, seeming unable to hold something in any longer, erupted in wildly excited words.

"I'm closing down next month," she

said with a big grin that spread all over her glowing face. "I'm selling out to Owen Williams. He called me today from his daughter's house."

Cassie stopped with the cookie halfway to her mouth.

"You're what—Rosie, but you said you'd live on your own bagels before you'd let him have your bar."

If possible, Rosie's grin got wider. "You've heard of offers you can't refuse." She laughed, a high, screeching giggle that made Cassie think of the Wicked Witch of the West. "I can travel or go live on Padre Island. I've always wanted to live on Padre Island. I might open a coffee bar there. And my boyfriend's going with me. Maybe he can find a place for his music shop when he quits that detective—" She stopped, suddenly seeming to realize that she had said too much. Then she quickly covered a silence between them with another gushing flow of words.

"Cassie, I know that buying me out means he's going to make a move on you. After all, you're between us. But, well, you're just barely here. You'll make a profit on a few weeks' work. It can't be any big deal to you." She turned to serve a woman who had come in, effectively closing off anything the dazed Cassie might want to say.

Cassie pitched her latte and cookie into the trash. She couldn't put anything into her shuddering stomach now. She carried Julia's drink back to her.

Julia was opening a packing box. She looked up briefly, carefully pulling out some straw packing and winding it around her arm before dropping it into the trash. "Your order arrived," she said, looking back into the box. "The dolls for that empty tree."

She pulled out a tiny doll and slipped it out of its plastic wrapper. Cassie set Julia's drink down on the register table and reached for the doll. The miniature doll was a true replica of earlier china-faced dolls, wearing an old-fashioned baby blue dress with lace around the neck and sleeves.

Cassie raised and lowered the doll, watching the minuscule eyes open and close. "That makes a kind of sense now, I guess," she said. "Now that Christmas is over and now that Rosie's given in."

Hesitantly, trying to keep the tremor out of her voice, she repeated Rosie's announcement.

"I'm as surprised as you are," Julia said, making a face as she took a sip of the hot drink. "Rosie has always been so tough on them and their ambitions." She stood with the coffee cup in her hand, looking serious. "Maybe too tough. I'm sorry, Cassie, if I listened to her too much. It seems now that she had her own ambitions. But we can't really blame her for all that, Cassie. Everyone makes their own decisions on what's best for them. She hasn't known you long enough to feel any loyalty. But I do blame her for using you to help her get what she really wanted."

Cassie whirled around to face her. "Mom—"

"Shhh, honey. We need a lot of ribbon to tie these dolls on the tree." She put down the drink and reached for the doll and slipped a ribbon loosely around it to hang it on the tree.

Cassie stood watching her for a while, feeling in some weird way that she was trying to decide which of the ideas, memories, whirling through her brain to give thinking room to. Finally, she simply started digging dolls out of the packing case.

They took turns unpacking the dolls and hanging them without talking much, each turning off their thoughts to concentrate on the best possible placement of the dolls.

"Should we move them closer to the front, do you think?" Julia asked when they could stand back and admire the tree.

"Maybe later," Cassie answered. "I planned it to be where customers would wander back and be surprised. And enchanted."

Julia nodded. "Good idea. I think it will work."

Cassie busied herself with arranging a basket of teddy bears on each of the steps that Little Bit had used to climb to the big bear's lap. After a while she was ready to talk about her latest disappointment.

"You don't have to explain Rosie to me, Mom. I know who to blame. And I'm not going to give in. This is my first business, and I'm going to make it a good one. They'll just have to walk around Teddy Bear's Shop to get to their new expansion."

Julia brought a handful of ceramic candles to place about the bears. "It almost makes me feel good to think about that. I know you'll win. But I'm sorry that this has turned out the way it has. I admit I thought Mitch was being low-down when I first came, but I was aware of something between you the past few days and I was slowly changing my mind about him. I'm still not sure of what is going on, but I'm sure that you will succeed in whatever you decide to do. I'm sorry that I have to go back to Dallas soon, but I do. Just remember that if you decide you don't want to stay where you'll be seeing him every day, you're welcome there. Anytime."

Cassie stuffed a last teddy bear in the basket. "I wish you didn't have to go back too, Mom. And thanks for the welcome, but I'm staying."

Someone came in then, and they both got busy. Cassie wished the day would never end, and people would never stop coming in. Every time she found herself with nothing to do, the thoughts of Mitch raced through her head, sending slashes of pain through her whole being.

Ian came in late in the afternoon of the next day. A day after a night in which the thoughts of Mitch's ruthless actions was almost touchable in Cassie's sleepless mind.

Ian barely took time to greet Julia or even say hello to Cassie. He didn't pretend not to know what had happened.

"Cassie, I need you to go with me. I'm Mitch's friend, but I'm your friend, too."

Cassie looked at him suspiciously. "You aren't going to try to make me go over and make up with that man? Because I won't."

Ian shook his head. "Not directly."

He refused to tell her more. He made no move to stop or even ask her to look inside the bookshop as they passed, though Cassie thought she heard Little Bit's loud complaints about being separated from his dear love. Wondering if Mitch was watching them go by, she still refused to allow herself even a glance toward where he would be—if he was watching.

"You aren't going to tell me where we're going?" she asked.

Ian didn't look at her as they maneuvered their way through the less-crowded, post-holiday River Walk. "We're going to La Villita."

"Why?"

"Wait." He seemed distant, his mind on something else. He was not the jovial easygoing man she thought she knew.

Some tourists looking for souvenirs in after Christmas sales wandered through the La Villita shops, but the gallery where Nerina's paintings had been displayed was empty. The woman who seemed to be watching the place nodded to Ian and went into a room behind the gallery when they came in.

"First of all," Ian said, pointing toward the disappearing woman, "she isn't involved in any of this. She just knows that Nerina and her paintings are gone, and she'll soon be finding another job. And I asked her to give us a few minutes alone."

Cassie looked at the empty gallery without interest. Nerina wasn't important any more. "Nerina? Why do I care if Nerina is here or gone?"

"You care, Cassie. Listen to me," Ian said, putting both hands on her shoulders. "Because Nerina is the one who paid that man to get the miniature back. She didn't want you to have it. She wouldn't have sold it to Mitch if she'd been here that night. And she paid the man extra to trash your shop."

Cassie removed his hands and walked to the window, shaking her head. "Good try, Ian. I admire you for being loyal to Mitch, but I know what I heard. He said that the people next door paid him."

He came to the window and stood beside her, not touching. "Think a minute, Cassie. Exactly what did he say?"

She was silent, watching the stream of

casually clad people walk by. She let herself recall the scene scorched so vividly in her memory, yet kept a step away by her own mind in order to not totally devastate her spirit. "I asked him if it was the people next door who paid him, and he was coy. He was sounding all the time like it was no big deal. It was a huge deal to me."

Ian put his arm around her. They watched the thin stream of visitors outside.

"Cassie, remember exactly what he said. Exactly."

"Ian, you sound like a psychologist on a TV show. Of course I remember exactly what he said. He said there might be some connection. Does that answer your detective soul?"

His mouth stretched, but the exuberant Ian grin just wasn't there, and the strange expression in his eyes didn't change.

"I can give you a better answer. The

connection was jealousy. Nerina wanted you to leave and get out of Mitch's life. She was upset that your shop hadn't been totally trashed when the police came. Cassie, Mitch didn't have anything to do with it."

"How could you know that? Of course he's going to tell you he wouldn't do such a thing."

"Nerina told me. She wouldn't talk about it yesterday, even when I came to the gallery and found her hiding the painting. But she admitted it to me today in a call from Mexico. She's scared."

Cassie looked around, something inside her afraid to accept what Ian was saying. That Mitch wasn't part of that horrible night, that he hadn't caused the horrible nights to follow.

Now she absorbed the bare walls of the gallery. "That's why all her paintings are gone?"

"All but this one." He took the miniature out of his pocket. "She told me where it was. She thinks no one can really prove she ordered the trashing since Harmonica Man is way somewhere else now, but since the painting belonged to you, she could be arrested for paying him to steal it. Just in case, she's staying in Mexico for a good while. She will tell me where if I should choose to follow her later."

Cassie turned back to watch the people outside for a moment, while she was allowing the heady reality to shove out all her suspicion of Mitch. Ian was telling her the truth. Truth she should have seen for herself. Truth she should have allowed Mitch to tell her. It was too overwhelming to contain yet. She turned to Ian, letting his emotions ease her own. She slipped her hand over his.

"And you will. You will go to her."

He nodded. "I told you I would be there when she realizes who she needs. I love her, Cassie. And somewhere under those layers of personas is the real Nerina."

She took the miniature and studied it for a moment. Then she put it in his hand. "I'm giving it to you. What you choose to do with it is up to you. There'll be no charges of theft. She can stay in Mexico or come back to San Antonio."

"Why, Cassie? You can't be wanting to be good to Nerina."

She shook her head. "If I had Nerina here, I'd—I'd do something awful to her. I'm giving it to you. To thank you for being a good detective and a good friend." She flung her arms around his neck and kissed him. "For what you just gave to me."

He kissed her earnestly in return. Then he called out to the woman in back that they were leaving. Outside, he told her good-bye briefly. "You know the way back?"

She laughed. "All the way back. All the way back, Ian. Now I have to go apologize to my neighbor and make friends again with a cat."

14

MITCH WAS ON his knees beside his register counter, unloading a new shipment of books. He had several short stacks of brightly covered books scattered around him. He looked up but didn't move or put down the book he had in his hand when she burst in. His expression didn't change from concentration on comparing the books with the invoice on the floor beside him to either happiness or anger. His shoulders seemed to sag, though she wasn't sure she saw any actual movement.

The sudden realization that he might not welcome her after the terrible accusations she had made crashed against the soaring happiness that had made her seem to fly to him from La Villita like a lilting cloud. The abrupt change inside her spirit stopped her as if she had smashed into an invisible barrier that had reared up before her. She had to brace both hands against the counter to keep herself upright. For minutes that seemed like hours, they simply stared at each other across the counter. Then she accepted that the start of any discussion must come from her.

"Mitch, I'm sorry. I was wrong. I accused you of awful things. I was wrong." She felt as if she had to push each word of the request for forgiveness past something solid in her throat. The confession she would joyfully have made from the safe haven of his arms became an aching throb against the implacable look of his face.

Still he didn't move or change expression. "And what makes you think you were wrong?"

She felt a deep longing to tell him her

angry accusations after the burglary had been from the fleeting agitation of that moment, that she had had later thoughts, and that she came to believe in him on her own. She refused to give in to that desire, strong as it was. Only honesty would suffice here.

"Ian took me to La Villita. To Nerina's gallery. He told me what happened. That Nerina paid the man to steal the painting. To trash my shop. That she was the one who wanted me to leave San Antonio. That she was jealous. Because of you."

He nodded, still neither changing the position of his body as he knelt by his books nor relaxing the stiff muscles of his face.

"Your change of mind has nothing to do with any belief in me or my feelings toward you. Cassie, I love you, but I need more than your being shown proof that I wouldn't do such a malicious thing to you. What if some other bad thing should happen between us in the future? Would we go through this again? Would you stop believing in me again? This is important to me, Cassie. I thought a relationship was built on trust."

She longed to kneel beside him. To throw her arms around his shoulders. She moved one step toward him, then stood still, wishing she were not looking down on him, searching for any welcome from him for her to come down beside him.

She let her words, her deepest thoughts, come tumbling out. "Mitch, I know I've got a lot to make up, but think for a minute. I was panicking. My whole life was coming down. I accused you— down deep inside, no matter what I was saying to you—to my mother—and Rosie made it worse—no matter what, way down deep I was hoping you would show me that it wasn't you."

"And nothing changed until Ian changed it?"

She nodded slowly. "I let myself hold

onto everything I could. So I could be so angry I wouldn't admit I was hurting the way I was hurting. And what happened in my shop made all that Rosie's been saying seem so real."

"I know what Rosie's been saying. I hoped you weren't letting her get to you. I seem to have been wrong about that, too."

She felt a flash of anger again. "You could have told me. You could have talked to me. About whether or not you want my space."

He put both knees on the floor and leaned back. "Perhaps I should have. Perhaps I was unfair not to, to want you to believe I wanted the best for you because of the feelings growing between us. But would you have listened? To me or to Rosie? I tried to tell you with my actions, but you saw everything I did through Rosie's gossip."

"Rosie's selling out to your father."

"So she is. He wants to get her out of here. She's causing too much trouble."

"He can afford to buy someone out just to get them to go away?"

"He can. He's a businessman. Someone like Rosie takes away from the mood of the Walk. Customers can feel it. And we suspect it was Rosie who wanted your space. For her boyfriend to sell CDs. His private detective business is failing. She thought she could discourage you by blaming me. She didn't expect me to fall in love with you."

Cassie was silent for a moment digesting this. A blip of memory of an overflow caused by cotton balls in her sink, of a wild purple coffee stain on her carpet, and Rosie's presence, slipped through her mind. Then she realized that it wasn't important any more. But getting some uncertainty out of her mind was.

"You have to get my space if you're going to expand."

"I said my father is a businessman. The string of stores he's looking into here in San Antonio need much more space than we have here. He's going to open away from the River Walk."

In a heartbreaking moment, she watched him turn away from her and pick up a book.

"Are you satisfied now? Have I explained enough?" His voice seemed to come from miles away. From the place where her suspicions had sent him.

Cassie looked at him in silence for a moment. "You just said you love me."

He dropped the book in the floor, and stood up. "Of course I said I love you. I've been trying to tell you I love you since about the first time we fought over Little Bit. I told you I love you when I showed you the river in the morning, when I took you to see where your angel was, when I nagged you into the band. Most of all when I kissed you."

"Doesn't love mean when I say I'm sorry, you forgive me?"

He shook his head. "Forgiving has

nothing to do with this, Cassie. Forgiving is easy. There has to be trust."

Looking at him, she knew there was nothing more she could say. Fighting tears, she turned to walk out, hoping to keep some kind of dignity. But there was one thing that had to be sure between them. She looked over her shoulder to see something that shone like tears in his eyes as he watched her walk out, a silent movement of his hands toward her. One honest thing. She had to say one last honest thing.

"I love you. I trust you enough to tell you I love you while you're sending me out of your life." She didn't stop walking toward the door.

She didn't see Little Bit deciding to come out of hiding and wrap his squashy body around her feet until too late. She heard his snort of abuse as she trapped his body between her feet and stumbled across the floor, fighting to stay more or less upright all the way. She caught the doorjamb and righted herself before going out onto the Walk, no longer fighting the tears but letting them wash down her face. She'd not only been sent out of Mitch's life, she had lost all dignity in exiting.

"Cassie. Cassie. Are you all right? Cassie, wait. Look at me."

Hallucinating. That was what she was doing. Mitch, of course, was over beside his books watching her with no expression on his face, or concerned about Little Bit, who might be stretched out dead so that Mitch would know that she didn't bring anything but evil into his life. She kept on walking.

She felt him catch her shoulder from behind. She turned to see his face closer to her own than she could have imagined. She simply stared at him for a moment.

"Are you all right, Cassie?" His deepened voice told her that he cared.

She mentally reviewed all parts of her

body. "Just a few pulled muscles. You're checking on me? Before Little Bit? Or have you already checked him out?"

"Little Bit is smarter than I am. He tried to keep you from leaving. I'm not saying he knows that I'd be sorry for the rest of my life if I let you go, but I know I would. Will you forgive me for refusing your apology so insufferably? I wanted to make you hurt just because I was hurting. Please come back in. I want to kiss you. I want to tell you again and again that I love you."

Without words, she turned back with him, and let him lead her to his shop. Inside, she moved to him, her hands cupping his face, slipping over his hair, her mouth rising upward to his even before she felt the welcoming sensation of being pulled into his arms, the union of his lips on hers. This kiss was a bonding, a celebration of their declaration of love. She felt more tears on her cheeks but now they were comforting, a letting out of the pain of a short time before, almost like the tears at a wedding.

Several delightful minutes later, he lifted his head and touched his hand to her face.

"Does that answer all your questions? Can you be more generous than I was, and forgive me? Cassie, I love you so much I thought I would die from losing you."

She nodded, not feeling any need for words.

He laughed softly. "Then perhaps we should continue this later, since my front door is open. You're sure nothing is hurt except some muscles?" His voice got deeper. "You're sure you meant to say you love me?"

This time she searched his lips with hers, and he let her answer his question with their touch against his. Finally she drew away.

"I'm sure about me. I'm sure of everything about me. Physical, mental, heart to toes." She laughed from pure happiness. "How about Little Bit?"

"Little Bit tore out of here ahead of you as soon as he got away from your feet. I'm betting that he's already in the lap of your bear, licking his imaginary wounds."

She sighed, not wanting to leave his arms. "And I should go there, too. Mom is trying to pack today, and I've left her in the shop too long."

"Cassie, can she stay long enough for us to have an early dinner together?"

"Come with me. We'll ask her."

They found her mother watching in disbelief as Little Bit snuggled into the lap of his favorite bear. It took a lot of excited explaining before Mitch flicked the CLOSED sign on his shop and went for take-out, before Julia admitted, perhaps a little sorrowfully, that they had misjudged Mitch.

"And do we add Owen to our list of people we misjudged?" she asked at the end of Cassie's story. Then, "Did you know how Ian felt about Nerina?"

"Some. He'd talked a little. I know when you first came down you hoped that it would be Ian and me, but we were never meant to be anything more than friends and part of the band. We'll miss him in the band, but maybe he and Nerina will come back when he gives her back her painting."

"Is there some way the police should be brought into this? After all, no matter who paid the man, it was a crime."

"Ian promised to give them enough information to let them close the case. I doubt they consider it enough of a crime to try to bring Nerina back. After all, only the value of the painting could be considered theft, and I got that back, and then gave it back. The damage here was small, thanks to you calling the police. No, I think it's over, Mom, unless they should happen to find the harmonica man, and who knows where he may be now."

"And you don't believe that Mitch wants your space, much less Owen?"

Cassie hugged her mother. "I only believe that when Mitch was angriest at me, he said he loves me. I think that is what happens in a good relationship. That you still love someone even when you're fighting. True? I used to run somewhere when you and Dad had a big screaming fight, not because I couldn't stand the fight but because I couldn't stand your gooey-ooey, smoochy making up."

Julia smiled, pulling away and going into silent memories for a space. "Okay, baby, you've told me something we didn't know before. We always shut up and settled down to work it out when we realized you'd disappeared because we were afraid we'd leave you branded somehow." She returned Cassie's hug. "Thanks, my wise, even as a child, daughter. I really must leave tomorrow. But if you're close enough to the Earth to watch the shop while I go up and pack, I'll take over while you have dinner with Mitch. Maybe Sarah and Danny can take care of the bookstore."

Cassie expected a dinner at one of the outdoor cafés on the River Walk, but instead Mitch took her to a restaurant in the city proper, where they were ushered into a private room. The room was empty except for a table set for two with champagne and candles.

She looked at him with a smile of pure happiness, which turned to mischief. "Are you sure you're not setting this up to make me an offer on my shop?" she asked, feeling a final lifting of some weight she had been carrying since the first time Rosie had spoken of the grand conspiracy.

He grinned back, waiting until the maître d' lit the candles and poured two glasses of champagne. "Well, no," he said then. "I was trying to set up a place to ask you to marry me."

She looked at him silently for a long time. "I wish you had asked me on our bench by the river."

The expression on his face sent her into laughter. He joined her briefly then called the maître d'.

"Please have the waitperson pack our dinner. We've decided to have a picnic."

The maître d' was surprised into looking at them in disbelief for a moment. Then undoubtedly expecting anything from two people so obviously in love, as well as a pleasant tip, he called the chef and several waiters, who efficiently packed up the entire menu that Mitch had pre-ordered and carried it to his car.

A half-hour later, Mitch opened up a small table from his shop in front of the bench they would forever call theirs and covered it with a folded linen cloth. He unpacked the food, lit a fat candle on the walk in front of them, and poured the champagne. Cassie watched him happily, knowing that both Sarah and Julia knew they were there and were probably enjoying their presence with frequent phone calls to each other, though they would never interrupt them. Cassie neither knew nor cared if Rosie or her boyfriend knew they were there.

Passersby glanced at them, then quickly looked away, as though somehow aware of an aura about them that was not to be disturbed, even if two people sitting on a sidewalk bench, eating lobster bisque from delicate china and drinking champagne from crystal glasses, would ordinarily have caused more questions.

They ate in contented silence, watching the glorious sunset colors. At their height, he put his glass down on the sidewalk. Ignoring the fact that it promptly fell and spilled champagne beside them, he turned to her.

He sat only looking down at her for several moments.

"It's been a long time to have been

such a short time I've known you, Cassie. I thought my life was good with the shop and the writing and the music. You whirled me around so fast I'm still dizzy. Dizzy with loving you. Dizzy with how much better you've made my life."

Cassie chuckled. "You left out Little Bit. I'd ask you to drink a toast to him if you hadn't spilled your champagne." Then she sobered. "I thought you were making my life worse for so much of this long time. And I fought with myself about my feelings for you. But all the while they were there. All the while."

His arms came about her. "I don't need champagne. I just need you. Cassie, I love you. Will you marry me?"

Ignoring the people milling about and now looking at them with indulgent smiles, mostly guessing what was happening between the two, she threw her arms around him and answered with her kiss.

15

"MOM, I'M NEVER going to get this dress into that carriage," Cassie moaned, twisting to see as much as possible in the full-length mirror that Julia had hung on her bedroom door for this day.

Julia, looking lovely in her own simply flowing blue gown, stood back and surveyed Cassie with satisfaction. "You look beautiful. Like a perfect model of a June bride. You could be on a cover. We'll help you get in."

"We? You and Sarah will be busy getting your own dresses in, and Mitch isn't allowed to come near me till the wedding, whoever made that silly rule. We should have just slipped down by the river with our work clothes on and married ourselves, and then told everyone later."

"And not let me plan my only daughter's wedding? What kind of reward is that after nine months and all those hours in labor? What do you think we mothers go through all that business for? For planning the wedding, that's what for. Stand still for a minute. I need to get this thing on right." Julia indicated the tiny bead encrusted tiara and swaths of veiling she held ready to place on Cassie's head.

Cassie moaned. "It's so fancy. It doesn't seem to fit anywhere on my head." Then she grinned. "Okay, Mom, I admit that somewhere under my business suit a big part of me wanted a romantic wedding. I remember playing wedding when I was little. I remember you playing with me."

Julia stopped moving the headdress from place to place on Cassie's head to look beyond her for a moment. "I don't think we ever played wedding in a church that looks like a store, though. Now why don't you sit down so I get a better view of the top of your head? And," she held the headdress up to admire it, "this does make you look like the princess that you are."

Cassie reached up and placed the tiara on her head in the most comfortable spot. "But that's exactly where this wedding should be if it can't be by ourselves down on the Walk. In Sarah's church with the band there. And some churches might not want the ceremony the way I want it. This is the dream I had even if I didn't know it."

Julia settled the headpiece a little closer onto Cassie's head. "I've been afraid sometimes that we've kept Mitch from really courting you with all our meetings about the store plans. I hope you don't feel cheated."

Cassie laughed, looking at the amethyst-encircled diamond on her hand. "I suppose I should take this off now," she said dreamily. Then, "No one has ever felt so courted in this whole state, maybe in this whole world. Even when we were all sitting in Owen's new store planning ours, I felt Mitch's love. And," she added, smiling contentedly, "we weren't always with you. And, Mom, having you in the coffee bar is going to be wonderful. Especially when we have the walls cut out so it's all one big store. But I think I'm maybe more excited than Mitch is about bringing Sarah into the bookstore so he has more time to write his stories. He's dedicating all the stories to me. It makes me feel as if he's giving me the River Walk."

Julia nodded. "I think people will love it. Bookstore with music, Christmas and other things, and coffee and goodies, and a working writer somewhere around. What's not to love? I talked to Helen again last night. The lawyers have the agreement ready, and she's ecstatic about leasing my Denver store. So happy that I'm coming down here."

Cassie took one last look at her gracefully swirling dress. "As is one Owen Williams."

"I hear the horses outside," Julia said, hastily. "We mustn't keep them waiting. Are you sure your headpiece is on solidly?"

"If you don't touch it again." Cassie hugged her. "I do feel like a princess, Mom, but then I would have if we'd slipped down to the river. So long as it's Mitch."

Julia nodded a smiling agreement. "But, now, let's see if we can get this dress out the door and into the carriage without letting it drag."

Sarah, wearing a gown fashioned like Julia's, but in a soft lavender—"Symbolic of a happy, peaceful life for you and Mitch," she had told Cassie when they were discussing wedding plans—came in from the other room where she had discreetly found something to do to give Cassie a last moment with her mother.

Together they lifted the trailing folds of Cassie's gown to keep it pristine.

Owen waited on the street with the two carriages. "I know Mitch can't see the bride, but I can," he said, hugging her very carefully before helping her into the carriage. He helped Sarah and Julia into the second carriage before getting into his car to be with Mitch at the altar when they arrived. As she settled into her carriage for the ride to the church, Cassie felt an added soft happiness to see that the horse was the one that Mitch carried carrots and apples in his pocket for.

At the church, while the bridal party waited for their cue music, Cassie glimpsed the inside of the sanctuary. It was just as she wanted it, with simple garlands on each pew and the altar decorated with candles already burning on standing holders with trailing flowers skillfully draped about them. She had chosen not to have ushers or to seat anyone on a special side. Everyone there was friend of both the bride and groom and had chosen their own seats when they came in.

Keith and Benny stood beside the piano, holding their instruments. The church pianist stopped the soft music she had been playing and let a moment of silence quiet the church, then swung into the happy bridal music. Cassie, holding a simple nosegay of daisies, placed her hand on Julia's bent arm and watched Danny march proudly down the aisle carrying the two rings on a pillow. After he took his place at the side, Sarah walked down the aisle. Then she and Julia stepped out, Cassie never taking her gaze away from Mitch, standing tall beside Owen, watching her come to him.

At the altar, the young minister asked, "Who gives this woman in marriage?"

"I do," Julia said, "with the love of her father." Instead of sitting down, she remained beside Cassie while Sarah went to stand beside the piano to sing a wedding medley, accompanied by Keith and the piano, with Benny weaving notes into their music to add to the mood. After she sang, Sarah came to stand beside Julia.

Mitch and Cassie had chosen to use the classic vows rather than write their own, promising to love and honor each other. When the ceremony ended and they turned as husband and wife for their friend's greetings, Cassie saw Ian seated with Keith and Benny in the back of the church. How had he heard in Mexico, and what a pleasure to have him come. He gave her a special hug when he went by the reception line and whispered, "Your wedding was every bit as good as my own."

During the reception, which was catered in the decorated basement, he filled them in on his life in Mexico, while Keith and Benny played soft music. "Nerina has decided to go back to being the person she really is," he said. "She even considered changing her name back to Martha, but I discouraged that. Nerina sounds good for the very excellent paintings she's doing, concentrating on the old Mexican civilizations. I brought some of them to open her gallery in La Villita again. Some day, Cassie, she will come back to San Antonio, and you will get to know her as she is."

In spite of the good will and happiness in the day, Cassie couldn't imagine wanting to meet Nerina again. Mitch came to her rescue.

"Ian, there's another guitar. You don't think we'd let you get by without playing?" Ian grinned and joined them.

After the toasts and celebrations Cassie noticed Sarah and Julia quietly passing out tiny baskets of bird seed, and she prepared to run the gauntlet to the carriage that waited to carry them back to Mitch's car, packed to take them to some undisclosed honeymoon place.

At the carriage, Julia gave them both a last hug. "Don't give it even a thought on your honeymoon," she said, "but when you get back, those doors will be cut in the walls and Teddy Bear's Shop will be one big store."

When they were settled into the carriage, with their favorite horse clipping down the street, Cassie turned to Mitch, a mischievous glint in her eyes.

"See, I knew all along that you wanted to get the Teddy Bear's Shop space."

He cupped her cheek in his hand and looked at her for a moment with complete delight showing in his face. He kissed her. It was a soft kiss, drifting from the corner of her mouth to the corner of her eye, but telling her how much she was loved, whispering of the depth of their shared happiness.

Then he answered seriously. "No, Mrs. Williams, all I really wanted—from the first day I stood outside Teddy Bear's Christmas Shop door and you wouldn't let me in—was the shop's owner."

About the author

LOUISE COLLN WRITES in Franklin, Tennessee, where the natural beauty and sense of history encourages her interest in people, and appreciation of the world we live in. This is her fifth book.